"Sunny..." Raj breat... warning. "Marry me.

Sunny blinked and stared incredulously back at him. "Raj..."

"I mean it. I don't want the three of you on a sporadic visiting basis. I want you all permanently. Marriage is the logical next step forward for us and it will overcome many of the irritations currently making your life difficult. If you're my wife, I can shield you from all such annoyances. I will not have you depicted in the press as some temporary occupant in my bed, a target for insinuation and rumor. Nor do I want my child becoming a target."

He closed his hands over hers and tugged her closer.

"You've shocked me," she whispered truthfully, shaking her head as if to clear it of the mental fog that had engulfed her.

BABY WORTH BILLIONS

LYNNE GRAHAM

PRESENTS

**Harlequin®
PRESENTS™**

Recycling programs for this product may not exist in your area.

ISBN-13: 978-1-335-93898-5

Baby Worth Billions

Copyright © 2024 by Lynne Graham

Harlequin Enterprises ULC
22 Adelaide St. West, 41st Floor
Toronto, Ontario M5H 4E3, Canada
www.Harlequin.com

Printed in Lithuania

MIX
Paper | Supporting responsible forestry
FSC® C021394

Lynne Graham was born in Northern Ireland and has been a keen romance reader since her teens. She is very happily married to an understanding husband who has learned to cook since she started to write! Her five children keep her on her toes. She has a very large dog who knocks everything over, a very small terrier who barks a lot and two cats. When time allows, Lynne is a keen gardener.

Books by Lynne Graham

Harlequin Presents

The Italian's Bride Worth Billions
The Baby the Desert King Must Claim
Two Secrets to Shock the Italian

The Stefanos Legacy

Promoted to the Greek's Wife
The Heirs His Housekeeper Carried
The King's Christmas Heir

Cinderella Sisters for Billionaires

The Maid Married to the Billionaire
The Maid's Pregnancy Bombshell

Visit the Author Profile page
at Harlequin.com for more titles.

CHAPTER ONE

Raj Belanger, the richest man in the world, was in a reasonably good mood as his helicopter landed on the roof of the Diamond Club in London.

After all, the exclusive club, a sanctuary for him and other people of immense wealth, was his personal creation. Lazlo, the manager, greeted him quietly at the door and ushered him indoors to the welcome quiet of the private members' club. The classical décor of marble columns and high ceilings matched with muted colours and the ultimate in opulent comfort was satisfying to Raj's critical gaze. And within the refined safe harbour of the Diamond Club, there were no paparazzi or celebrity spotters. The staff were rigorously vetted and trained. Every member enjoyed a private suite and the catering and business facilities were as international as the clientele.

Encountering an appreciative appraisal from Lazlo's female assistant manager, Raj looked away, his dark golden eyes reflecting irritation at the height, build and dark good looks that had always attracted too much attention to him. Six feet four inches tall, he was a lean, powerful, strikingly handsome man, who despised vanity. He stayed fit for the sake of his health and stamina. He believed that what was inside an individual was a great deal more important than their outer shell. Beauty faded, but without disease, intelligence survived. A former child prodigy of unequalled brilliance and a legendary entrepreneur in the fast-moving tech world, Raj had strong opinions and few people dared to argue with him.

His British lawyer, Marcus Bateman, awaited him in his private suite. A small, grey-haired man, he had an astute brain and shrewd business sense. As breakfast was set out for them, Raj made small talk because he never discussed private matters when there were potential witnesses present. Once they were alone, he broached the issue that had troubled him for longer than he would have cared to admit: the plight of his orphaned niece, Phoenix Petronella Pansy Belanger.

Four months earlier, Raj had lost his last surviving relative, his brother, Ethan. Ethan and his wife, Christabel, had died in a car crash. A cocaine-fuelled car crash. The nanny looking after their ten-month-old baby girl had immediately contacted social services, keen to hand over responsibility for her charge and find a new placement.

'Have you changed your mind about seeking custody?' Marcus enquired quietly.

'No, if Christabel's half-sister is deemed a suitable parent for the child, I have no objection,' Raj declared levelly. 'As a single man, I would be the wrong guardian for a little girl. The life I lead is wholly unsuited to childrearing, nor would I even know where to begin in that task.'

The older man nodded, aware that Raj had been subjected to a dysfunctional environment from when he was an infant until he was finally emancipated from that regime by his mother's desertion of his father. Raj's own disturbing experiences would make it almost impossible for him to relate to an ordinary child. In truth, Raj had never known what it was to be ordinary. He had been hothoused and home-schooled and had won a handful of advanced degrees from the world's leading universities long before he became a teenager.

It was in the normal affection and social stakes that Raj had lost out most. He had been raised without warmth or friends and with parents whose sole focus had been on developing his exceptional intellect. When his mother had given birth to Ethan, however, Raj had been naïvely thrilled by the prospect of a kid brother. Protected from their father's malign influence, Ethan had been raised with everything that Raj had been denied. He had been cuddled and encouraged, loved and praised even when he hadn't deserved it and yet, much to Raj's dismay and surprise, Ethan had somehow matured into an appalling failure. Had his brother been spoilt? Had the umbrella of cash provided by Raj's wealth caused Ethan's expectations to range too high? Had the unfair comparisons made between the two brothers cruelly damaged Ethan's ego and backbone?

Raj had done everything within his power to support his brother as an adult, particularly after his mother's demise. Sadly, Ethan had failed to rise to the challenge of the many opportunities he had been offered. Indeed, Ethan had proved to be weak, lazy and dishonest, although his disloyal and greedy wife, Christabel, had been the worst of the two. Raj had met his niece only once at the christening font when she had been a red-faced and screaming little bundle and he had had an accidental glimpse of her once in the hall of his brother's home. Further meetings after that had proved problematical because neither Christabel nor Ethan had liked social occasions with young children present. The baby had been kept very much in the background of their lives and Raj suspected that she had seen more of the nanny than she had ever seen of her parents.

'Miss Barker, the child's aunt, has agreed to allow you to visit your niece,' Marcus told him cheerfully. 'I took the liberty of consulting your PA and organising an access visit for next week.'

Raj thrust his breakfast plate away and thanked him. 'But I gather that the foolish woman is still refusing to accept any money from me?' he murmured flatly.

'She remains determined to raise the little girl without your financial help,' Marcus confirmed. 'It's admirable in the circumstances.'

'Irrational,' Raj overruled impatiently. 'I will address the issue when I meet her next week.'

'Bear in mind that Miss Barker is not in need of money. She's a successful artist in her own right. Arguing with her could cause resentment and make it more difficult for you to retain access to your niece. In a few months the adoption will be ratified by the court,' Marcus warned gravely.

Raj compressed his lips. He foresaw no difficulty in dealing with Sunshine Barker. Had he believed that she bore the smallest resemblance to her late sister, Christabel, he would have felt forced to dispute her application to adopt their niece. But he had had Sunshine's life extensively researched and she was as different from the unscrupulous and calculating Christabel as it was possible to be. She lived in a country cottage and embraced the rural life right down to the extent of foraging in the local woods for cooking supplies. She was educated, creative, bohemian, a messy blonde in Moses sandals with a string of rescue animals. But she was also well respected in her community and well liked.

Raj did not see her as a challenge.

Sunny had dropped her contact lens and she couldn't find it, although in the process of feeling delicately over the floor and below furniture she had discovered a hairbrush and a brooch that she had thought she had lost. In frustration she fumbled for her spectacles on the nightstand by the bed but she had evidently mislaid them as well, which was unfortunate when she was virtually blind as a bat without them. They would turn up, sooner or later, she consoled herself, screening a yawn as she brushed her mane of blonde hair with the retrieved and now dusted brush.

She was tired, naturally, she was. Just yesterday she had had Pansy stay overnight for only the second time and now her niece would actually be living with her round the clock. Even so, she was still being vetted as an adoptive parent by the social services and another orgy of cleaning and tidying awaited her because, while nobody expected her to live in a perfect household, a slovenly one wouldn't be acceptable either.

It was just unfortunate that Sunny hadn't yet had time to complete her renovation of her late grandmother's cottage. She had had the bathroom and kitchen gutted soon after her grandmother's demise six months ago, but the walls still rejoiced in ancient chintzy wallpaper and her own clutter was now layered over both her mother's and her gran's cherished bits and pieces. She was looking forward to plain painted walls, but the original pine floors were a little cold and hard for a baby who was starting to walk, so she had put down fluffy rugs for her niece's benefit. Eventually, she would get the house fully sorted but, right now, Pansy's care, comfort and contentment were her main priorities.

And now this wretched insurance assessor was coming to view the barn, which had been damaged by a storm ten days earlier. She suppressed a sigh, relieved that her niece was down for her nap and that she had contrived to dress in her version of an office worker's clothing for what she viewed as a formal meeting. It was true that the skirt was a little tight... too many bacon sandwiches when she was short of time and energy, and possibly too many chocolate treats at the railway stations she had hung around in while she was commuting back and forth to London on a daily basis to get properly acquainted with her niece at her foster home. Familiar guilt at her poor food choices trickled through her. And the long-sleeved top felt a little neat too over her bountiful bosom. Sunny much preferred loose garments in soft, misty colours like the plants she adored.

The bell went in three short hasty bursts. *Three!* Good to know upfront that she was about to deal with an impatient person, indifferent to the presence of pets and a baby in the household. Bear, her Great Dane–wolfhound mix, loosed a bone-chilling howl, making her grateful that she had no close neighbours. Barefoot, she sped to the door, afraid that tardiness might affect her claim.

A very tall male towered over her. She focused on a shirt button visible between the edges of a suit jacket and then a tie and was relieved that she had put on the skirt and top.

'So, you're...er...whatever. If you would give me just two minutes, I'll slip on my shoes and take you round to inspect the barn...'

The shoes she had intended to wear were still in the bedroom but her trusty welly boots were by the wall and she thrust her feet into them instead. 'These will do,' she said with a wide smile, skimming a glance up and up...and up. 'My goodness, you're very tall.'

'You are...petite,' Raj selected with unusual tact, although he was really wondering why on earth she wanted him to inspect her barn.

He was transfixed by her because she was such a mess. Her skirt was lopsided and unbuttoned at her tiny waist, above which swelled the sort of splendid feminine bounty that Raj generally only saw in his fantasies. The ugly orange top looked like something dragged out of a charity shop and the skirt was covered with animal hair. A faint shudder of distaste slivered through him but his dark gaze stayed welded to the huge smile lighting up her face. She was gorgeous, undersized and over-endowed in curves it was true, but still undeniably gorgeous. She had the most amazing tumbling fall of long wavy golden hair and violet eyes the colour of a flower, not a person, he adjusted. Coloured contact lenses? No, she didn't seem the type and she had yet to even look him in the face.

'Do you have any identification?' she asked him, something Raj had never ever been asked before.

His hair was dark, well, she was almost certain of that but he was only a blurred vision of size. He was way too tall and broad and kind of intimidating in stature. If you were the sort of woman who *was* intimidated by large men, that was…and she was *not*.

She didn't recognise him? Raj was amazed. She had not been at the christening or the wedding. However, he had somehow assumed that she had been at the double funeral. Admittedly though, there had been a huge turnout for the funeral, and he had not met her then, probably because he had been surrounded by people too eager to speak to him and ensure that he noticed their presence and remembered their names. He should've made a point of meeting her that day, he castigated himself. Unfortunately, he had kept his distance from the group of Christabel's friends, many of whom had been taking selfies and photos and generally conducting themselves as though they were attending some glitzy event, rather than a tragic interment.

Suppressing a sigh, he withdrew his passport and extended it. Sunny Barker had the tiniest fingers he had ever seen on an adult. He was hugely entertained by the whole process as she squinted uneasily down at the passport. She was irredeemably scatty, badly needing to be organised by someone. She would drive a control freak of his type insane, he reflected absently.

Sunny peered down at the passport but it was just a blur and she thought it was a very odd means of identification to show her. Hadn't his insurance firm given him an identity card with a logo? Evidently not and that was scarcely his fault. It was not as though she were inviting him *inside* her home, she reminded herself soothingly.

'Your barn?' he prompted with rare indecision, willing to play along to be reasonable and reluctant to embarrass her, which would only increase the awkwardness of their first meeting.

'Come this way,' Sunny urged, squeezing out past him—really, he did take up an awful lot of doorstep space—to lead him down the path and round the corner of the house into what had once been a farmyard.

Bear gambolled along by her side, giving the visitor a very wide berth. Bert peered out and snarled from beneath a shrub they were passing. Bear backed away. Bert advanced, threat in every line of his tiny body.

'Stop it, Bert!' Sunny scolded. 'You're being a bully.'

Raj glanced in disbelief at the tiniest dog he had ever seen outside a handbag. The giant dog was terrified of the tiny one. He wondered why he was being shown the barn. He wondered why he was with this strange woman, who didn't even recognise who he was. Did he expect everyone to know him at first glance? Sort of, he acknowledged uneasily. And Sunny Barker was his former sister-in-law's sibling, shouldn't she recognise him? Have taken some interest in his presence in the family tree? Even if they had never enjoyed a formal introduction?

'So, here's the barn. As you can see a giant branch fell on the roof and messed it up a little.'

'More than a little,' Raj countered, studying the poorly maintained structure, automatically foresee-ing any insurance firm's likely response to such a claim but stifling his urge to issue a warning. In-stead, he viewed the very tall horse staring out at him over the stable door. 'Who's this?'

'Muffy. She's a Clydesdale,' Sunny told him, sud-denly full of animation, delighted, it seemed, by his presumed interest. 'She was very upset about the roof tiles falling and the rain coming in.'

Raj contemplated the misnamed horse, who didn't look as though she would stir into life for anything less than a hurricane. 'She seems content.'

'She's very easy-going…but I need the roof fixed. She's elderly,' Sunny whispered, as if the horse might be shy about her age being bandied about in public. 'She needs a nice dry stall.'

'Why are you showing me your barn?' Raj chose to ask abruptly, watching as she petted the horse, the movement drawing the top tighter over the ample swell of her breasts while he wondered why he was even looking.

Anyone would be forgiven for thinking that he was a teenager who had never seen breasts before! For goodness' sake, he was a sophisticated male with four mistresses in different cities. He took care of his sexual needs in the same efficient way that he took care of everything else in his life. He focused on pri-vacy and practicality. He could be in London, New York, Paris or Tokyo and he could lift the phone and

visit any one of his mistresses. Reminding himself
of those facts did nothing to prevent his intense gaze
from sliding from the generous thrust of her breasts
to the curve of her perky and curvy bottom as she
bent over the door and then angled those violet eyes
up to open very wide on him. Unforgettable, beautiful eyes.

'Why are you asking me that? You're an insurance
assessor,' Sunny told him in surprise.

'No, I'm not. I'm Raj Belanger and your niece is
also *my* niece and I've arrived on a prearranged visit
to see her…'

'You're coming to visit *next* week,' Sunny informed
him with confidence. 'Same day, pretty much the
same time but definitely *next* week.'

'I think you'll find you're incorrect in that conviction. My staff rarely make mistakes,' Raj asserted
drily just as the shaggy Great Dane bolted from behind his owner to flee behind Raj in a determined
effort to escape the domineering, aggressive chihuahua.

Disconcerted by the sudden pandemonium, Raj
suffered a glancing blow to the back of his legs and
skated forward, belatedly discovering that the surface below him was slippery and giving his soles no
purchase as he was thrown off balance. He fell back
heavily into the mud and lifted himself even faster
to stare down at his soiled hands in disgust.

'I am so sorry…' Sunny whispered, urging him
by the elbow back towards the house, thinking that

the bigger people were, the harder they fell, but she had never seen anyone look quite so appalled by a little mud. 'Come this way, so that you can wash.'

She had been about to tell him that he had arrived on the right day but in the wrong week, only it seemed unkind to make that comment just at that moment. Was this man truly Pansy's uncle? The richer than Croesus guy? She was appalled at the reception she had given him. Of course, he had been quiet. He had been wondering what on earth she was talking about but had been too polite to say so.

Raj was already using his phone with angry stabs of a muddy finger, speaking into it in another language in curt tones of command. He was kind of bossy and he had a short fuse, Sunny decided as she got him back through the front door and spread open the bathroom door to the soundtrack of Pansy wailing for attention. 'You'll want to…er…freshen up and I'll bring you a towel.'

Yanking fresh towels in haste from the laundry press, she laid them on the hamper by the door and tried not to notice that he had clearly fallen into a puddle because his suit trousers were wet and mired. Poor man, as prone to accidents as the rest of humanity in spite of all his wretched money, she reflected ruefully, ashamed that she had had many unkind, biased thoughts about him in recent weeks. A male who apparently believed that he could *bribe* her to take *better* care of his niece, apparently incapable of understanding that she most wanted to be a mother to Pansy and simply love her. And there would be no price tag involved in that process.

Someone was knocking on the door again. She sped to answer it, wanting to go and lift Pansy but determined to take care of everything at once. Another formally dressed male handed her a suit in a zipped clothing bag. 'For Mr Belanger,' he told her.

She wondered where he had come from and how he had arrived with her so quickly but she was flustered now and she raced back to thrust the bag at her visitor and swiftly closed the bathroom door on him again to go to her niece's room. Pansy was standing up bouncing at the side of the cot. With her mop of blonde curls and big blue eyes, she was incredibly cute and she lifted her little chubby arms to be lifted as soon as she saw her aunt.

'Yes, my precious. Aunty was late,' she confided softly, sweeping the soft warm weight of the toddler up into her arms and hugging her close. 'Time for your snack…right?'

Raj surveyed the modern washing facilities with intense relief as he stripped. He had enjoyed disturbing glimpses of other rooms en route to the bathroom. And everything was flowery or patterned and there was clutter on every available surface. The cottage was a hoarder's dream and he could see that the knick-knacks were creeping in to despoil the bathroom as well. A line of pottery flower sculptures adorned with improbably sparkly fairies marched along the window sill and he raised his brows.

Raj liked order, reason and discipline in every space he occupied. Everything, outside the arts, had to be functional in his world. He stepped into the shower because he was soaked through to the skin and the hot water soothed him even if the soap's strange grittiness did not. He was in Sunny's home, accepting her hospitality, and it would be strange not to expect differences, he reminded himself. *She* was different, after all. *Very* different, he conceded thoughtfully.

Towelling dry and feeling rather more like himself, he got dressed again in the fresh suit and put the discarded one in the empty bag. After a moment's hesitation, he lifted the discarded towels and placed them on top of the laundry hamper. For the first time in many years, he was making an effort to be scrupulously polite.

'Mr Belanger?' Sunny called as soon as she heard the bathroom door open. 'We're in the kitchen!'

Raj breathed in deep, like a male girding his belt before battle, and, pausing to acknowledge the threat of the low doorway, he ducked his proud dark head and strode on into the kitchen where bunches of wizened foliage hung down from the rafters. His attention, however, shifted straight to Sunny and her welcoming smile before almost apprehensively moving to the child seated in the toddler high chair. A pretty little girl waved her toast at him happily while slurping clumsily out of a toddler cup.

'Sit down at the table and make yourself at home,' Sunny urged expansively. 'I know you haven't had much contact with Pansy—'

'Pansy?' Raj interrupted in surprise. 'I thought she was called Phoenix. And any official documents I've seen on her refer to her as Phoenix.'

'Apparently your brother preferred Pansy and told the nanny to use that name,' Sunny told him. 'And the social worker in charge of her case decided that was best because she already recognises her name. The other two names are a bit…fancy.'

'Interesting,' Raj remarked, duly informed. He had thought the names a mouthful as well but prided himself on being too diplomatic to express that opinion.

'Coffee or tea? I have a lovely soothing herbal tea.'

Raj didn't believe he needed soothing. 'Coffee for me, black, no sugar, thank you. And call me Raj. In a loose sense, we are members of the same family,' he opined.

Warmed by that unexpected acknowledgement of a family link, Sunny poured the coffee, set it in front of him and slid over a plate of biscuits. 'Help yourself.'

Raj scanned the biscuits that had what looked like real flowers set into the dough. They were very decorative. He breathed in deep and selected one.

Sunny laid a knife on the plate. 'They're all edible

flowers but if you don't like the look of them, feel free to scrape them off,' she said lightly.

Raj ignored the knife and chewed the biscuit, which tasted surprisingly good. He watched Sunny lift his niece from her chair, clean her up carefully and then begin playing with her.

'Who's a beautiful girl, then?' she asked the baby, who was in the air chortling with glee, bare feet kicking up.

As Sunny turned her face up to look at the child, her expression shone with love and warmth and happiness. It was exactly what Raj had hoped to see in the woman who wanted to mother his orphaned niece and he was pleased and relieved in equal parts. 'What made you decide that you wanted to adopt her?' he heard himself ask.

'I'm unlikely to have children of my own. I have a…medical condition,' she admitted uncomfortably. 'And there was Pansy alone without parents and she's my own flesh and blood. It was an instant decision. I only wish Christabel had allowed me to visit her more often and then I would have been more familiar to Pansy when I came back into her life. Instead, I had to get to know her as a stranger.'

'Why didn't your sister allow you to visit your niece?' Raj enquired with a frown.

'Well, my half-sister and I weren't close. She was eight years older and then we grew up apart.'

'That's right. I seem to remember Christabel mentioning that her mother died and her father remarried and divorced.'

'And then last year, my grandmother, who owned this house, died and left it to me because this is where I grew up. Gran was terminally ill,' Sunny explained. 'Christabel took me to court to claim a share of the house's worth after my grandmother passed away and I'm afraid she was furious when I won the case. It also emptied my savings account, though.'

Raj frowned because he had read about the case in her background file. Her late sister had been remarkably avaricious, he mused, because, after marrying Ethan, she had not known what it was to be short of money.

'May I ask why you *didn't* want to adopt Pansy?' Sunny prompted.

'I believe that you have more to offer her,' he said quietly. 'I have no wife and no real desire for offspring. I wouldn't know where to begin raising a little girl and I would be reluctant to leave her in the care of a nanny all the time. My lifestyle would not be suitable for a young child.'

'You know your own mind and capabilities best,' Sunny conceded lightly. 'Speaking for myself, I'm grateful that I wasn't in competition with you.'

'Were I, at any stage, to consider you an inappropriate guardian, I *would* challenge you for custody. I should be candid on that score,' Raj incised, delivering that warning without hesitation.

Temper sizzled through Sunny at that arrogant

statement. Although *he* had no desire to take personal responsibility for his niece, he expected to sit in judgement over *her* parental skills. With difficulty, she stifled her resentment, determined not to get on bad terms with such a powerful male. 'I'm happy that you have enough interest in Pansy to visit her. She won't have a father but, hopefully, she'll have a favourite uncle.'

'That's generous of you, although I expect to be only an occasional visitor.'

In a sudden movement, Sunny broke off listening to his well-modulated drawl and sped across the kitchen to pounce on the spectacles reflecting the light coming through the windows. 'I've been looking for these everywhere!' she gasped in satisfaction as she unfurled them and fixed them to her nose. 'I lose them so easily that I always keep three pairs on the go.'

'There are pairs of spectacles sitting on the hall-stand and also on the bathroom window sill,' Raj disclosed to her astonishment.

And Sunny was amazed by his observational powers and also struck almost dumb by her first proper look at him. She had seen his picture once in a newspaper and had thought that he was an attractive man if a little grim and grave of expression. But in the flesh, she learned that Raj Belanger had much greater impact on her as a woman. He had stunning even features, high cheekbones, an aristocratic nose and a wide full mouth. His face was further blessed by very dark, intense eyes surrounded by dense inky lashes. Gorgeous, simply gorgeous eyes.

'You're staring at me,' Raj said sardonically.

'I'm sorry. You just look much more handsome in person than you do in a newspaper when you're always looking forbidding,' she mumbled. 'And you don't look at all like Ethan.'

Dark colour scored the line of Raj's high cheekbones. 'You don't really think before you speak...do you?' he countered.

'It's a habit of mine. I'm sorry for getting so personal and embarrassing you.' Now equipped with her spectacles, Sunny, with cheeks burning fire-engine red, studied the calendar on her wall and her slight shoulders dropped. 'And I owe you another apology. You were expected today and the insurance assessor *is* coming next week. My only excuse is that I've been getting ready for Pansy to come home and I've been very busy.'

Raj waved a forgiving hand, grateful that they were off the topic of his appearance and her barn. Did he look forbidding as she had termed it? It was true that he didn't smile very much. Yet wasn't it strange that Sunny made him want to smile because she amused him? She was all out there like an advertising hoarding while he was the exact opposite, generally keeping his feelings to himself and of a much more introverted nature.

'Let's move into the sitting room so that you can start getting acquainted with Pansy,' Sunny suggested, lifting the plate of biscuits and his coffee and her own tea onto a tray.

Raj vaulted upright, feeling as though he were being managed and disliking the unfamiliar sensation. He watched Pansy toddle somewhat clumsily in her aunt's wake, very much like a miniature drunk struggling still to find her balance.

He was smiling when he followed the duo into the cluttered sitting room where piles of books, potted plants and, in one corner, an actual log made the small space seem even smaller. He sank down into an armchair. He studied Sunny, who was gazing owlishly at him from behind her spectacles. That blue-violet shade of eyes had a luminous quality, he decided. His attention lingered.

'Why does Pansy not know you either?' Sunny asked just as Raj was about to ask out of sheer curiosity why there was a log on the floor.

'I generally only saw my brother and your sister at adult social occasions. I entertained them at my London home but they always left the baby at home,' he explained. 'Your sister said that she needed a break from being a mother. Why weren't you at the wedding or the christening?'

'Christabel had a simply huge guest list of important people she had to invite and I didn't make the cut and our grandmother wasn't well enough,' Sunny said without chagrin. 'I did understand. She and Ethan led very glamorous lives in comparison to ours.'

As Sunny brought a plastic container of toys out and Pansy began noisily tossing everything within it out, Raj relaxed a little because he was not immediately being challenged with the task of getting to know a young child. 'Where do you do your painting?' he asked curiously.

'In the sunroom behind the kitchen. The light's good there. I usually get up at the crack of dawn to paint. But I'll have to adapt my schedule to suit Pansy now.'

Encountering a narrowed glance from his dark eyes, which flamed gold in the sunny room, Sunny could feel her self-consciousness rise exponentially. There was something very intense about Raj Belanger. She didn't know whether it was the raw, restive masculine energy he emanated or the demanding potency of his dark gaze. But there was definitely an unnerving quality to being in his powerful presence. She could feel her nipples tightening inside her bra and a faint uncomfortable clenching in her pelvis. She went rigid, suddenly registering that what she was feeling in his radius was not simple tension but pure sexual attraction. It had been so long since she had experienced such a reaction to a man that she was sharply disconcerted by it.

'I'd like to see your work,' Raj declared, breaking free of the odd spell she cast over him to withdraw his gaze from her. What the hell was the matter with him? In denial of the stirring hardness at his groin, he turned his handsome dark head away to watch the large black cat pad from behind the potted plants, where he had evidently been sunning himself, to claw at the log. 'Who's this?'

'Miracle…the only survivor of a litter who died, a bit like Bear. Bear's mother rejected him at birth. I brought him home to see if I could feed him and keep him alive and, as you can see, he survived.' At the sound of his name, the big dog approached her and pushed against her knee affectionately before lying down, the very picture of relaxation.

As Pansy saw the cat, she let out a squeal of excitement and reached out her arms. The cat sprang off the log and ran out of the room and Sunny laughed. 'Miracle already knows to stay out of her reach. Bert stays in his basket in the kitchen. Hopefully he'll be adopted this week. A lady is coming to see him. He needs a home where there are no other pets or children.

'I'll show you the studio,' Sunny added, rising up, allowing her niece once again to toddle in her wake.

He followed them into the sunroom, a large unexpectedly clear space dominated by an artist's easel and a side table stained with paint and littered with sketches, photos and brushes.

'It's not finished yet,' she explained as he looked over her shoulder at the watercolour.

'*Anthriscus sylvestris* aka cow parsley,' Raj murmured, amazed by the detail she had already brought into being.

'Or Queen Anne's lace, which sounds much more

romantic,' Sunny pointed out. 'Although that's actually a different plant known as wild carrot.'

'What do you work from?'

'Sometimes photos, sometimes the actual plant, sometimes both. You know the Latin names.'

'Yes. It was a hobby when I was younger. I liked the precision of Latin plant names.'

Sunny stepped away from the canvas, surprised by the intensity of his scrutiny when she had expected him to show only a cursory interest in her work.

Raj loved the watercolour. It was so real he felt as though he could reach into the picture to touch the delicate lace blooms and it was a much more scientifically accurate presentation than he had expected from her. 'Let me buy it,' he suggested suddenly.

'I can paint you another one but I can't give you *this* one,' Sunny declared in a surprised rush. 'It's the last of a series I've done for a big botanical book that's soon to be published and I'm tied by contract to hand it over.'

'Who would ever know that you gave this one to me and another to them?' Raj asked drily.

'I would know and that's not how I work with my clients,' she retorted crisply.

'I'll commission you for another,' he responded curtly, dissatisfied by her reluctance to cater to his request, a response that he had never met with before. 'Am I allowed to ask why you won't agree to me providing financial support for my niece?'

Disconcerted by that sudden change of subject,

Sunny hovered uneasily, her heart-shaped face troubled as she struggled to put her convictions together in a hurry. 'I don't want Pansy to be so spoiled that she no longer follows her dreams or strives to achieve something of her own in life. Ethan was like that. He knew he could have virtually anything he wanted because you would buy it for him or make it happen for him, and it only made him impossible to please and it stifled any natural drive he had.'

Raj gazed down at her in complete shock, colour slowly receding below his naturally olive complexion. Nobody had subjected him to such blunt speech or censure since childhood. He was stunned by her lack of tact and her daring in mentioning his late brother in such terms.

'Who do you think you are to speak of my brother in such a manner?' he shot at her in a sudden burst of anger.

It wasn't a shout; he raised his voice only a little but his intonation was raw and the atmosphere was tense. Pansy was standing by the window, and her little face crumpled and she loosed an uncertain sob. Sunny reached down to lift and comfort her niece. 'I think it's time you left,' she said tautly.

Firm mouth compressed, Raj did not require encouragement to take his leave. He was outraged by what she had said about Ethan. She seemed impervious to the awareness that, as the giver of that money, Raj would not accept being blamed for having encouraged Ethan's faults. He had simply done his utmost to find some field that interested his brother into making an effort and the sad truth was that he had failed. Leaving Ethan to sink alone had been too much to ask of Raj's conscience. Every time he had failed with Ethan, he had tried again…and again.

He strode to the front door and opened it, breathing in slow and deep. 'I will see you next month,' he announced. 'Same day, same time…if it suits you.'

'It suits,' she conceded, white as a sheet as she watched him stride down the path and heard a vehicle engine start up and then another engine, indicating that more than one car had accompanied him to the meeting, but any cars were hidden from view by her high hedge.

Listening to the cars recede into the distance, Sunny groaned out loud. Oh, what had she done, speaking so candidly on such a private, personal and decidedly hurtful topic? Of course, he had taken offence when he had done his utmost to settle his brother into a secure position! And she had only got to know Ethan through his visits with Christabel before their wedding, because there had been little contact after that date. She should have more carefully chosen her words, lied if necessary, she reasoned unhappily, rather than risk antagonising Pansy's uncle by referring to his sibling like that. Instead, she had waded in, careless of the wound she might be inflicting, and she was ashamed. Yes, she had spoken her true feelings, but honesty was not always the best policy.

CHAPTER TWO

'IT'S NOT LIKE you to make a personal call at my home,' Raj told his British lawyer in surprise, two weeks later. 'Has some catastrophe occurred?'

Marcus chuckled and extended the large wrapped tube he was carrying. 'It's for you…from Sunny Barker, I understand. As she doesn't know where you live or have your phone number, she asked us to see that you received it and her letter.'

Raj tensed as he accepted the tube. 'Letter?'

Marcus moved forward to settle an envelope on Raj's tidy desk.

Raj ripped open the envelope with scant ceremony and pulled out the single sheet. He was stunned to realise it was an apology and a generous one, even if her wording made his wide sensual mouth compress. Had she really needed to tell him that she was sorry she had hurt his feelings? He wasn't an adolescent boy in therapy. No, she didn't have tact but what she did have was the sort of honesty that Raj had never met with before and decided integrity. It wasn't a grovelling apology either. She didn't disclaim the views she had voiced, merely acknowledged that she should have had more sensitivity and that such 'unkindness' was not the norm for her.

Raj opened the tube and, with great care, drew out the coiled watercolour within, a sizzling smile flashing across his mouth as he unfurled it to see the painting she had refused to sell to him. He carried it over to the window to check that it was not a copy, but no, she had done what she had said she would not do and had given him the original because he remembered some tiny marks at the edge.

'That relationship is progressing well, I assume,' Marcus gathered.

'We had a…difference of opinion at our first meeting,' Raj admitted reluctantly.

Marcus raised his brows in surprise. 'That must have been interesting.'

Raj nodded. He was already wondering where he could obtain a scratching post for a cat. It would get rid of that unseemly log. She had offered an olive branch. Raj was keen to be equally generous because he wasn't proud of his own behaviour. He became exasperated but rarely did he ever lose his temper and yet he had almost lost it with Pansy's aunt. He had brooded over that anomaly ever since that incident. Sunny Barker had unsettled him and he didn't like it. He had had to resist having the last word by making a second visit. That would be childish and he was never childish. Furthermore, any reopening of that controversial topic would have entailed discussing his relationship with his brother and he had no intention of violating his own privacy to that extent.

Clutching Pansy to her bosom like a magic talisman, Sunny clambered clumsily out of the helicopter onto the tarmac before being guided across to the private jet. *One* of his jets, she reminded herself dizzily, not his personal one, just simply one of a fleet. She couldn't comprehend that level of wealth. It was simply too overwhelming but, if she wanted to support her niece having a relationship with her rich uncle, common sense told her that she had to suck it up.

Raj had responded handsomely to her gift of the painting he had admired by inviting her and Pansy out to his home in Italy on the Amalfi coast. They were both trying to forge a familial relationship for a child's sake and she didn't want to screw that up a *second* time, especially not when the social worker in charge of her adoption application was delighted that she was making that effort with Raj. That had brought home to her as nothing else could have done that she was stuck with Raj Belanger in their lives. Stuck with a guy who set her teeth on edge with his arrogant, far too clever ways.

The jet interior was amazing. As soon as she stepped onboard a woman in a uniform asked to take Pansy. 'I'm Maria. I'm the nanny engaged to give you a break, Miss Barker,' she was informed.

Afraid her mouth was dropping open at such an announcement, Sunny watched her niece being carried to the rear of the cabin. Pansy was sociable and quite happy with people who were equally friendly. Recalling the complete lack of contact between Raj and his niece on his previous visit, Sunny felt guilty for throwing him out of her home. She had never done anything of that nature in her life before but that was, unhappily, a result of his effect on her. And why was that?

She *knew,* of course she did. In some weird way, Raj reminded her of the male who had once been the love of her life: Jack. Jack had been tall and broad too, the *very* masculine, outspoken type. For once, Sunny allowed herself to take those painful, youthful memories out. Jack, who had told her he loved her, had dumped her the day after she told him that children were an unlikely possibility in her life. They hadn't been lovers, for she had been only seventeen, but she and Jack had grown up together, had been childhood sweethearts. Even now, she still had to see Jack every week at church, where they acknowledged each other with a distant nod as he settled his wife and many children into their family pew.

'It means you're not really a proper woman any more,' seventeen-year-old Jack had told her, striving to justify his decision. 'I'm sorry but I want kids in my future, *my own kids*, not adopted ones or surrogate ones…or however you were hoping to *trick* me into marrying you!'

So, that had been that, the bitter end of a rosy adolescent idyll, but Sunny hadn't put herself out there to be hurt again. She had a fatal flaw and she had accepted it, made her peace with it, but she wasn't ever going to place herself again in a position where a man could dismiss and belittle her as Jack had. The burst appendix that had almost killed her at the age of twelve had wrecked her fertility prospects and there was nothing anyone could do about that reality. No matter how much that truth hurt, she had to live with it. She never had got the chance to tell Jack that she had got that same news from her poor mother only the night before she told him. Petra Barker had lacked the courage to make that truth known to her daughter *before* she reached seventeen.

Wiping her brain clean of those memories of disillusionment and pain, Sunny studied the botanical and animal magazines being brought to her with amusement. Yes, Raj already knew better than to bless her with fashion journals. Really, he was too clever for his own good, she reflected wryly. Did he think she hadn't guessed that he must have had her investigated by some private security firm? Raj Belanger was not the type likely to leave anything to chance and she was not stupid.

An opulent limo collected her from the jet and bore them off to their destination. A huge mansion that could have been a palace awaited her and Pansy at the end of a long imposing drive, guarded by giant wrought-iron gilded gates and security personnel.

Sunny refused to be impressed. Raj inhabited another world, that was all. Money was money and it didn't necessarily make people any happier. She based that assumption on Ethan and Christabel's visits before their marriage when family ties had still been acknowledged. Their only conversation had related heavily to Ethan's misfortunes in business, Christabel's supposed sacrifices and complaints, their possessions and the famous celebrities they socialised with. Listening had made Sunny want to shout that they were two very lucky people and why couldn't they appreciate their health, youth, attractiveness and good fortune in being gainfully employed? After all, it was much more than many people had.

Sunny bent down to let Pansy put her feet to the ground in her first proper shoes and she wondered if Raj would notice that his niece's ability to walk had hugely improved. She was urged through the imposing front entrance into a vast space filled with marble, glittering crystal chandeliers and art works on plinths. There was absolutely nothing welcoming about it. It was an environment that could only influence and intimidate. Raj stood in the middle of it, looking about as friendly and as remote as a towering dark monolith on the moon. Pansy shrank against Sunny's legs, her little body trembling.

'Raj…' Sunny said simply. 'What a beautiful home you have…'

But that wasn't really what she thought, Raj guessed, because her expressions were easily read. Presumably she hadn't expected him to welcome her into a grass hut built in the wilderness, so why wasn't she questioning her own unreasonable responses? he wondered. She was biased against him. The money? Was that truly the only stumbling block between them?

It wasn't even as though *she* tried to fit in anywhere. She was wearing a sort of hippy throwback outfit in a soft blue colour that was so loose and shapeless that an elephant could have climbed inside it with her. He wondered what *that* was about and then questioned why he was wondering. After all, he had only dragged her all the way to Italy because it would be good for Sunny to appreciate that she would not be the only one calling the shots in the future. She was a damned managing woman and she needed that reminder. And, last but not least, he had fabulous gardens here that he assumed she would enjoy.

'You're in ideal time for lunch on the terrace,' he announced. 'I hope your journey was comfortable.'

'It was perfect. You make everything perfect,' she conceded, out of breath as he cupped her elbow with one hand to steer her out of the giant hall. 'But you haven't said hello to Pansy yet.'

'How can I say hello to a baby?' Raj enquired brusquely.

Ignoring that response, Sunny dropped down into a crouch and spoke to the child. Pansy waved her hand at him. 'You see…she can say hello!'

'No, she can't, because she can't actually talk yet,'

Raj pointed out grittily, dropping very reluctantly down to say softly, 'Hello, Pansy…'

''Lo,' the baby said distinctly, taking him very much aback with that ability.

'Hello, Pansy,' Raj murmured, a sudden smile of acceptance flashing across his firm lips.

Sunny watched in satisfaction because he had finally taken notice of the sole reason she was in Italy: her niece. But, my goodness, that smile of his was remarkable head-on, transforming his far too serious features into a darkly handsome face filled with a disturbing amount of charisma and sex appeal. A little tremor slivered through Sunny's taut frame, infiltrating places she didn't like to think about too much. It was physical desire and she fought that response to the last ditch.

He swept them out onto a tiled terrace with a magnificent outlook over beautifully maintained gardens.

'May I?' Maria, the young woman in a nanny's uniform who had been onboard the jet stepped forward and bent down to engage Pansy with a toy. Sunny released the child's hand and watched without surprise as her niece was conveyed down to the high chair sited at the far end of an extremely long table. *This* was how Raj worked with children in his vicinity, Sunny recognised. See a child, provide care and corral it where it could cause the least possible disruption. It was disheartening and it didn't leave her much room to work on his detachment. Unaware of her exclusion from adult company, Pansy waved at her aunt cheerfully and giggled.

'She seems to be a happy little creature,' Raj remarked with satisfaction.

'She is, and wonderfully adaptable because she takes interest in everything and everybody,' Sunny commented as pleasingly decorative salad starters arrived for them. 'I believe she's intelligent, may even take after you.'

'God forbid!' Raj cut in with an undeniable shudder of alarm at such a possibility.

'No, I didn't mean that I believe she could aspire to your level, only that she shows all the signs of being reasonably bright,' Sunny disclaimed in haste.

The tension in his broad shoulders and set features eased. 'I misunderstood,' he conceded, finally lifting his knife and fork to begin eating.

'What caused your...er...consternation?' she asked, curiosity alight in her vivid gaze.

'You would have to sign a non-disclosure agreement before I could answer that question,' Raj stated calmly. 'What little of my life can be kept private, I guard fiercely. I'm discreet and careful in my personal life.'

Sunny's eyes were wide and she nodded slowly in comprehension and agreement. 'I can understand that.'

Only what would remain with her for far longer was the emotional pain that had briefly shadowed his haunted dark eyes. She reckoned that his distrust of others possibly dated back to when he had been young and vulnerable. How many people he had had faith in had betrayed him back then? He was an extraordinary male in every way, who had probably paid a steep price for his brilliance, success and wealth, who had suffered in spite of it or maybe even because of it. She knew that reams of gossip and rumour accompanied his every move in public, but had never paused to imagine what it might be like living in such a goldfish bowl of constant attention.

'I'll sign one,' she conceded ruefully, recognising the necessity in his case.

Raj treated her to a slow-burning smile of approval that lit up her every pulse point and raised goose bumps on her arms. Heat flushed her cheeks, a warmth of awareness she could not suppress. Self-conscious, she concentrated on her meal, only to be surprised when barely a few minutes later a document arrived on the table and a pen was extended to her.

'Standard stuff,' he told her, flicking the fat document with a long forefinger in dismissal. 'But since you're likely to be in my life for years, I was hoping you would agree to an NDA as it makes life smoother and makes it easier for me to relax with you.'

Sunny rested back in her chair and skimmed through the document, aware of the older man at her elbow, presumably present to act as a witness. Feeling even a little pressured, she wondered if she should ask to take the document home with her and then she just lifted the pen and signed, foreseeing no future day when she would wish to reveal anything personal about Raj Belanger because she had always respected other people's boundaries.

Raj was stunned by the ease with which she had signed the NDA. People usually quibbled over terms, holding out to the last minute, invariably awaiting a financial reward for their signature, but Sunny had done none of those things, had sought nothing for her own advantage. All of a sudden Raj was in an unusually good mood, although he was thinking that Sunny needed a good legal advisor to protect her, which was an unusual thought for him around a woman. He didn't understand why but he knew the second thought that assailed him was that, *now*, he could kiss her.

Lust, he assumed, although lust had never dug such talon claws of need into him before. Indeed, he had believed that possibly he was not the most sexually rapacious of men until Sunny had strolled her messy but gorgeous self into his radius. And only then had he appreciated that something about this particular woman lit him up into a positive bonfire of sexual hunger. He had not gone a single day without thinking about her since that first meeting.

'So, I gather that now you will feel free to tell me why you believe a high IQ is a…a *burden*?' Sunny prompted over the main course.

'Not to everyone but it was in my case,' Raj asserted. 'My father was a brilliant and famous professor of psychology at Oxford when he met my mother, Clara. She was his brightest student and he seduced her at the age of eighteen.'

'I thought there were rules about that sort of thing.'

'Even then, there were. He resigned and returned to Hungary, and he took her with him while at the same time taking advantage of her ample trust fund. He used her, just as he eventually used me. She was already pregnant, and she had no family, nobody more mature to warn her that he was an abuser,' he admitted with distaste. 'But she looked up to him, admired him, believed he would know best about how to raise a child.'

Sunny winced, sensing she was unlikely to enjoy what he was on the brink of telling her.

'He, on the other hand, merely wanted a guinea pig for a science experiment on which he planned to write a book. *I* was that experiment from birth and he took copious notes on my every failure and achievement. I was raised in isolation, and I was only ever rewarded for the very best educational results,' Raj imparted levelly. 'I never played, I never had fun, my mother wasn't allowed to comfort or hold me. My father believed that the more I was deprived of, the more I would shine to try and please my parents.'

'Oh, dear,' Sunny whispered, pushing away her plate, her appetite killed by his confidences. Her empathetic brain was filled with horror at all that he had been denied as a child and her heart overflowed for him.

'I don't want your compassion, Sunny,' Raj told her warningly, recognising the glimmer of tears in her beautiful eyes. 'I only told you because I can sense your dissatisfaction with my attitude towards our niece. But you need to know first-hand that I *can't* play with her, *can't* show her affection when I have not the first idea of how to do such things…and that is why *you* will meet those needs for her that I lack the capacity to fulfil.'

'Of course, after such cruelty, you're going to think that, *feel* that way…' Sunny framed, luminous violet eyes swimming with an amount of emotion that somewhat unnerved him as she leant closer to him.

'But you can be fixed,' she told him, even more disturbingly, as though he were a broken kettle.

Her floral scent washed over him, soft and warm like her and, oh, so alluring on some level he didn't recognise. She was so close that he could count the three tiny freckles on the bridge of her delicate little nose and dwell on the soft full swell of her pink un-adorned lips. Raj went hard as a rock, his sex push-ing hard against his zip, a dangerously aggressive response for a male who had always believed that he could take or deny sexual impulses.

'I don't *want* to be fixed, Sunny,' he confided gruffly, almost laughing at that terminology. 'I've done tons of therapy and I am who I am and content with it.'

Sunny reached for the large hand braced tensely on the tabletop and clasped it tenderly and fervently between her own, little fingers smoothing over his taut fingers, thumbs caressing his wrist. 'But I can *teach* you how to play with her, how to show affection, and I'm more than ready to make that effort for both of you,' she swore vehemently.

'All I want to do right at this moment is kiss you,' Raj admitted darkly, fighting off the urge with difficulty.

Sunny blinked, finding it impossible to concentrate when he shot off topic to that extent. 'Why on earth would you want to do that?' she gasped in bewilderment, encountering mesmeric dark eyes that paralysed her where she sat.

'May I?' he stressed.

Shock claimed Sunny that he should be as attracted to her as she very much was to him. It had not crossed her mind once that that attraction could be reciprocal, but the knowledge of it now shone in the smile she gave him. 'If you think it would make you more comfortable with me.'

A very large hand reached out slowly as though he was afraid of spooking her. Long fingers stroked even more slowly down her neck to twine into her mane of golden hair and she stopped breathing, could literally feel herself stop breathing as if the earth had without warning screamed to a halt on its axis. She looked up at him with huge violet eyes.

'*Breathe*, Sunny,' Raj instructed hoarsely, enchanted by her reaction. 'Breathe before you pass out.'

CHAPTER THREE

SUNNY BREATHED JUST before Raj bent his dark head and covered her mouth with his.

And once again the world stopped dead, while her heart hammered and her body went off on a slew of discovery she had long since forgotten about. Nerve cells awakened from a lengthy slumber and a visceral response gripped her, heated energy pushing up from her pelvis and spreading like a dangerously contagious infection through the rest of her. Her nipples peaked with painful immediacy while a clenching sensation pulsed at the heart of her.

Raj tasted her as though she were the finest wine and he was determined to savour every tiny drop of it. His lips coasted back and forth over hers, coaxing them open, and then he was in and *she* was tasting him and every sense spun dizzily on a roller coaster of sensual discovery. His lips were soft and firm and the flavour of mint and man and the very scent of him left her light-headed. The first tiny dip of his tongue into her mouth was a revelation of skill because every inch of her responded with explosive force. As his hand closed round the back of her head in a possessive grip to pull her even closer, she was so overwhelmed by the sheer passion he had unleashed inside her that she yanked herself forcibly back from him.

Raj blinked slowly, allowing the world that had vanished to flood back in. That single taste of her had had the same effect on him as a rocket firing off and he had never felt anything that powerful with a woman before. Predictably, he instantly wanted more of it, *all* of it, all of *her*. Hard as a rock and unsated, he breathed in and out slowly, thoroughly tantalised by the revelation that there could actually be more to sex than he had always assumed.

Sunny rested a trembling hand down on the table to steady herself. She had never felt anything like that with a man before, not even with Jack, and it had shaken her inside out. But Sunny always looked before she leapt and she was immediately aware that she and Raj inhabited very different worlds and that he was Pansy's uncle, would always be Pansy's uncle. 'Well, that was—'

'Exhilarating,' Raj incised confidently, searching her hectically flushed face and the luminosity of her stunned gaze with satisfaction, knowing with certainty that she had been as affected as he was. No, she couldn't hide that from him and he liked that, no, he *loved* that. There was nothing studied or deliberately seductive or calculating about Sunny; she was simply Sunny. And he had never had that confidence with any other woman in his bed.

'Yes, well—' Sunny began jerkily.

'We'll spend tonight together on my yacht,' Raj decided, thrusting back his chair and rising to his full intimidating height. 'Let me show you the herb gardens now...'

Lord of all that he surveys, Sunny reflected, but thankfully not Lord of her as well. It was ironic that she had first wanted to laugh when he'd said that they would spend the night on his yacht *together* because Raj was making grand assumptions based on what was obviously the norm for him. One kiss and he assumed consent and agreement had been reached? That she would just fall into his bed immediately because he said so? Did she blame him for that? Or other women who had evidently gone to him far too easily?

As Raj reached out a hand to her to guide her down the flight of stone steps that led to the gardens, Pansy let out an ear-splitting screech and Maria scooped her up to try and quiet her. Pansy, however, fought the young woman, her arms stretching out for her aunt and a stifled sob escaping her. Sunny turned back and hurried along the terrace to reclaim her niece. Pansy lurched into her arms as though the poor nanny had been trying to steal her and, soothing her, Sunny walked her back to Raj, the nanny following.

'She's friendly with everyone but not surprisingly,

after recent experiences, she doesn't like me disappearing from sight in a strange place,' she explained quietly.

As a party of four rather than a party of two, they crossed the lawn. Raj's gaze had chilled and no longer glowed warm burnished bronze. Tough luck, Raj, Sunny thought, *she* comes first. Able to have Sunny close by, however, Pansy relaxed again and chased a ball.

'We need to talk about this…er…night on your yacht.' Sunny broached the subject with all the awkwardness of a young woman unused to such discussions, but one who had already grasped that, with Raj, subtle deflections wouldn't work. If left to reach the wrong conclusions, Raj would happily power forward on his own steamy assumptions.

'What's there to talk about?' Raj countered dismissively. 'We're attracted to each other, strongly attracted. Let's keep this simple.'

Sunny moistened her taut lower lip. 'But it's *not* simple. It's not as though we're dating.'

'I don't date.' Somehow, Raj managed to imbue that last word with distaste.

'Neither do I, as a rule, but I also don't jump into bed with strangers.'

Raj said something in another language that had the ring of a bitten-off curse word. 'I am *not* a stranger to you.'

'You're enough of a stranger to me that I have no intention of getting intimate with you. And what about the need for us to maintain a good ongoing relationship for Pansy's sake? Have you thought of how us getting involved could mess that up?' Sunny demanded succinctly, accompanying him below a rose-clad arch into a very private expanse, bounded by tall hedges. There she paused, enchanted by the vista of a lush, blooming herb garden with gravel paths and geometric beds.

'Oh, this is heavenly…' Sunny whispered, drifting away from him to explore as though she had seen some earthly vision of paradise and could see nothing else.

Unaccustomed to being forgotten about and disconcerted by her use of that particular argument on his niece's behalf, Raj wanted to yank her back to listen to him talk some common sense into her and he withstood that urge only with difficulty. He stalked after her, incensed by his rare failure to get his point across.

'So, I have to date you to have sex with you?' Raj loomed over her, blocking out the glorious sunlight.

'Don't be silly. That's not what I said,' Sunny replied. 'And if you're only interested in having sex with my body rather than *me*, just forget the notion.'

Raj breathed in so deep and long that she was vaguely surprised he didn't rise into the air with the pressure on his lungs. 'I don't understand.'

'Are you single?' Sunny asked.

'Of course I am!'

Sunny tipped her head back to look at him. That

violet gaze, some dangerous mix of pale blue and grey, rested on him with a remarkably sceptical quality. 'Are you seriously telling me that there are no other women of any kind in your life?'

Intelligence warned Raj to lie but he had never lied to any woman who shared his bed, had never allowed the smallest chance of a misunderstanding to occur. The women who entertained his leisure hours knew that they had a limited shelf life and that his interest eventually waned. He got bored quickly, always had, always would. He didn't get attached in any way. Sex was just another outlet, a harmless diversion and was usually no more important to him.

Sunny watched faint colour edge his high cheekbones and her heart sank because she had hoped that she was wrong and that there genuinely *weren't* any other women in his life.

'There are women…but not in the dating sense,' he framed with as much delicacy as he could contrive, hoping that she left the subject there.

Sunny's brows climbed as she continued to stare at him. 'Hookers?'

Raj was embarrassed, and he didn't think he had ever been so embarrassed in his life, and he couldn't credit that she could be digging to that extent or even that he was allowing her to do so. 'No…now let's leave.'

'Escorts?' Sunny cut in, startling him afresh.

'No.' Raj stared down into her feverishly curious

face and was startled to find himself on the brink of wholly inappropriate laughter. 'Mistresses.'

Her brow furrowed. 'More than one?'

Raj was done. He didn't even understand why he had answered her nosy questions. He jerked his chin in silent confirmation because no way was she getting one more word out of him.

'OK…' Sunny wandered away from him as though he hadn't spoken and began rhapsodising over a fall of lavender and the way the light falling on it created waving shadows.

She lived on another plane, an artistic plane, Raj acknowledged in frustration. At that moment he felt as though he had just had his insides dug out with a rusty spoon and he didn't know why that was so, yet she was sufficiently unaffected to admire the vegetation. That was why he didn't enjoy that comparison.

Sunny bent down to sniff the lavender and break off a piece and rub it between her fingers. Her eyes were still stinging with unshed tears. Mistresses in the plural. Well, at least he was honest about it, but it meant that *she* could never be with him.

'You don't seem surprised.' Raj hovered nearby, uncertain as to why he was reopening the wretched subject when he refused to discuss it any further with her. He only knew that he needed a response from her.

Sunny scrambled upright again, blinking rapidly. 'I'm not. It's practical, efficient…the sort of arrangement I would've expected from you,' she framed in a stiff undertone. 'Sorry, I pried.'

'You didn't. You asked and I chose to answer.' Raj reached for her hand but she tugged it away from him. 'What's wrong?'

'We shouldn't get close. We should work on being just friends…but not friends with benefits,' she hastened to point out in sudden mortification. 'I'm not the mistress type and I don't share, so, believe me, we're at a dead end here.'

Sunny was telling him that he couldn't have her, but Raj could not accept that refusal because he had never once met a situation he couldn't conquer or twist to his advantage. 'You don't share, so as well as dating you're talking about something exclusive as well,' he recapped with a frown of disbelief. 'That's not achievable, so we will have to compromise.'

'No more, Raj,' Sunny interposed gently. 'You know that you have no intention of compromising in any way and that you only expect *me* to compromise. I won't. I'm as stubborn as a pig when it comes to what's right for me…and for Pansy.'

'How do you presume to know me so well?'

Sunny gazed up at him, her own bewilderment at her conviction mirrored in her bright eyes. 'I honestly don't know how, but I do know that you're a very strong character and that you'll persist unless I'm firm.'

'*Firm?* I'm not a child, Sunny.'

No, she thought, he could do a lot more damage

to her than a child ever could. But he was, indisput-
ably, a raging storm of a male, accustomed to getting
his own way and capable of manipulation beyond her
worst expectations. Gut instincts served her well and
that was truly how she saw him. He was dangerous
to her peace of her mind and stability and her niece
needed a strong and steady parent.

And yet, on another level, she could still barely
believe that Raj Belanger, with all the many options
he must have, could actually want *her*. It was not as
if she were a supermodel or some sleek socialite or
sophisticate.

'We don't have anything in common,' she pointed
out quietly.

'We have passion,' Raj countered with immense
assurance. 'What more would we need?'

'If I have to spell out what more, we would be a
disaster…and anyway…' Sunny stood tall and lifted
her chin '…I don't want this. I'm happy with my life
as it is.'

'You haven't had me in your life before.'

Sunny dealt him a reproachful glance. 'This subject is closed.'

Raj laughed in genuine pleasure at that response.
Pansy surged up to his knees chasing her ball and,
without thought, he scooped up the ball and lifted it
above his head.

'No…throw it along the ground low or she won't
see it!' Sunny whisper-hissed at him.

Raj rolled the ball between the flower beds and

Pansy giggled and ran after it. 'She's much better on her feet,' he remarked.

Sunny smiled up at him. 'Yes, she's all change every day at the moment, moving from being a baby into being a real little personality.'

Her smile had the effect of making him smile and it irritated him because he was not pleased with her. She had handed him an ultimatum and Raj did not react well to ultimatums. In addition, she would now be chary of getting on the yacht in case he was taking them there for some nefarious purpose. Further irritation laced his big powerful frame. That particular problem, however, would be easily solved, he acknowledged as he pulled out his phone and made a quick call.

Sizing up the other issues, he questioned why he was trying to mix business with pleasure for the first time in his adult life. He never made that mistake. True, Sunny and his niece were not business, but they did not fall into the other category either. In fact, they had a category all of their own, somewhat filling that gaping space left by Ethan, that *family* space, he reasoned. Craving Sunny for pleasure was a messy, complicated desire. He compressed his firm lips. Logic warned him to suppress his hunger for her. But he didn't feel logical about Sunny. It wasn't rational or convenient to want her. There was simply something about her, some indefinable quality that called to him…*still* called to him even when she infuriated him. And it struck him as ridiculous that he, the ultimate cold-blooded, rational male, should appear, even in the trivial pursuit of sex, to have less common sense than eccentric Sunny.

He surveyed her and his niece. Sunny was kneeling in the gravel, showing a flower to Pansy, tickling her chin with it, laughing at the child's little giggle. The hippy dress already had grass stains and tracks from dusty gravel and she couldn't have cared less. Messy but somehow appealing for all that. Golden hair shining in the sunlight, luscious pink mouth pouting as she teased Pansy, her ever-ready smile beaming out. Warmth, he labelled, that was what she emanated like a forcefield. Warmth and acceptance and a kind of joy in ordinary life that was utterly fresh and new to him.

Sunny strolled back to the giant fancy house where they enjoyed fancy desserts and coffee on the terrace. It was downright magical with the fabulous view, the glorious weather, the food and the sheer glamour of it all, Sunny conceded, and it was exactly as Raj had probably planned it. The way she suspected Raj planned *everything*. There it was, that ridiculous belief that she knew how his brilliant mind worked. When he wanted something, he knew how to get it, never mind how unscrupulous his methods might be. After all, she was fairly sure that her visit had been planned as a long, slow seduction over lunch and drinks and glorious herbs in the sunshine. She might be naïve and inexperienced, but she was far from stupid.

'Tell me about Christabel as a child,' Raj asked her.

'Her mother died when she was quite young. She was eight when I was born, so I have very few memories of her because she was always away modelling or acting and my father was away with her,' Sunny confided. 'From what my mother told me, our father viewed Christabel as a superstar from the moment she won her first beautiful baby competition, which was before Mum's time with Dad. By the time they married, Christabel's star quality was Dad's sole interest. He gave up work to chaperone her when she started modelling in Paris at the age of fourteen and then she was starring in that TV soap opera that made her name.'

'You're giving me a different take on your sister. She was *pushed* into the public eye as a kid?'

'I think she was and our father acted as her manager. I only know that Mum felt as though our father married her to give Christabel a mother and then decided that he didn't need her or have time for a wife as well. She felt excluded. When Mum fell pregnant with me, Dad asked her to get a termination because he said they couldn't afford another child and that was the last straw for her,' Sunny admitted. 'They staggered along for another couple of years and then my gran was grieving so hard for my grandfather that Mum moved in with her. It was supposed to be temporary but it became permanent and my parents got a divorce in the end.'

'And what about your relationship with your father?' Raj prompted.

'It never really got off the ground. He visited a few times when I was a baby and then he passed away, so I didn't really know him, except through my relatives' opinions.'

'You were worth so much more than Christabel. She was as shallow as an envelope.'

Sunny winced. 'Maybe our father *made* her that way and taught her only to value her worth through her beauty and fame and earnings.'

'You always have that compassionate take,' Raj groaned as though she was paining him.

'None of us are perfect,' she argued. 'All of us have faults. You can't just judge people from afar.'

Raj groaned again. 'That's straight out of the Bible stuff…of course, you go to church.'

'Was it accurate, that investigation you had done on me?' Sunny enquired with unmistakeable amusement in her luminous gaze.

'Yes and no. The facts were correct, but the report didn't even catch a flavour of you as an individual,' Raj asserted without concern that she had guessed that he had had a private security firm check her out in advance of their first meeting.

She appreciated his honesty and was tempted to ask what flavour she was in reality, but bit her tongue instead lest he assume that she was flirting with him and digging for a potential compliment.

Later, they climbed into a motorboat to be taken out to the yacht, *Belanger I*, in the bay and she breathed in slowly, calming herself. Nothing was going to happen between her and Raj because an adult discussion had killed that possibility stone dead. What was wrong with her that, instead of relief, she was experiencing disappointment?

The truth was that Raj had wanted more and so had she, but common sense had prevailed. For the first time in years she had wanted a man and that recognition still shook her. She had shut down that part of herself after the disillusionment served by Jack. Jack had hurt her so badly at such a delicate age when she was still finding herself and she had gone through university specialising in turning potential boyfriends into mates, platonic mates. Yes, there had been presentable men back then, but none who had tempted her to try again.

Sunny shot a guilty glance at Raj as the breeze ruffled his luxuriant black hair above his bold bronzed, hard profile. A frisson of awareness ran through her, lighting her up inside like a shower of fireworks in the dusk skies, and she shivered. Almost instantly, Raj noted that shiver and stepped closer, peeling off his suit jacket and draping it round her, the silky warmth of the lining engulfing her arms and dropping to her knees, big hands resting briefly on her shoulders to steady her, and her tummy flipped as though she were on a roller-coaster ride. The scent of the jacket, of *him*, engulfed her, an indefinable scent that was just him: warm, male, laced with the faintest scent of cologne, and it felt so intimate that she shivered again.

Raj wrapped both arms round her. 'You're really cold. I'm sorry.'

Involuntarily, she encountered a look of surprise from Maria because it was a hot day and the breeze was slight. Her face burned even hotter. Raj made her feel horribly like an infatuated teenage girl.

Off the boat onto the massive yacht that she hadn't even had sufficient concentration to appreciate from a distance, she returned his jacket to him with a muffled thanks and took her niece's hand in hers to climb the stairs facing them.

'I'll carry her. The steps are too steep for her little legs,' Raj intervened and swept up Pansy without hesitation, bending down to murmur, 'Unfortunately, although your legs aren't much longer, I can't carry *both* of you...'

Reddening afresh, Sunny hastened upward and reached the top step to find a woman looking down at them all with a huge, bright smile. 'Welcome onboard,' she said in slightly accented English.

'Sunny, meet Bambina Barelli. She's an Italian *contessa* and a good friend.'

'I don't use the title these days, Raj...and no need for an introduction to this little girl!' The brunette reached for the child in Raj's arms with enthusiasm. 'You're Pansy, aren't you?'

And Pansy chuckled when, for the very first time, her aunt wished she would scream and act distant with a stranger. The meanness of that thought hit Sunny's conscience hard. Unhappily for Sunny though, Raj's 'good friend' Bambina was absolutely gorgeous, supermodel gorgeous with long swishy black hair, perfect features, almond-shaped dark eyes and legs that looked incredible in a short gold cocktail frock with diamonds glittering at her throat and ears. Sunny felt sick, her stomach swirling with nausea.

CHAPTER FOUR

'I NEED TO get changed,' Sunny framed, chin at an angle, eyes veiled.

'The stewardess will show you to your cabins…' Raj nodded to the hovering staff and watched Sunny, Maria and Pansy depart at speed. He frowned. He had assumed she would be relieved at Bambina's appearance but, if anything, the brunette had put her on her guard. *Az Isten szerelmere*, he thought in the Hungarian that had been his first language.

Sunny was like a string of computer code he couldn't interpret or guide in the most sensible direction. Weirdly rebellious against the norm that was what he deemed to be the average female response.

Their little group was shown into adjoining cabins. Pansy's rejoiced in a cot for a princess adorned in stupid drapes that would be dangerous for a toddler and Sunny and the nanny combined in silent agreement to remove the hazards.

'This is another…world,' Maria almost squealed in English, dark eyes wide and bright with excitement. 'And the opportunity of a lifetime. My mama will not believe that I was on board Raj Belanger's yacht with La Bambina as a guest!'

'She's a famous lady?' Sunny queried tightly.

And it flooded out of Maria. La Bambina was the Italian equivalent of a celebrity aristocrat from the very top drawer of Italian rich and famous people. She was never out of the gossip columns and as famous for her discarded husbands and lovers as her fashion sense. So, obviously, one of Raj's cohort of mistresses. What else could the woman be? Was she onboard his yacht to show Sunny what she had missed out on achieving? Well, so much for that loser game.

Once Pansy had had her supper, been bathed and tucked into the princess cot, Sunny went to change for dinner. No, she didn't have some gold cocktail dress tucked into a designer closet. She had an embroidered corset top with beads and long swirly skirt of equally handcrafted and beaded glory. It was very bohemian but she was comfortable in it, even if she did think that the neckline showed a little too much cleavage.

Go, Sunny, she instructed herself as she looked in the mirror, feeling horribly short-changed by nature, which hadn't endowed her with long legs or small, pert boobs or that slender designer silhouette that all models possessed. She was short and pretty dumpy when it came to designer comparisons. Indeed, just then it seemed a matter of wonder to Sunny that Raj should ever have looked at her with lustful intent.

Raj stalked forward to greet her in the huge salon, which acted as a reception area on the yacht. Sunny felt hugely self-conscious because she hadn't made use of the beauty salon appointment offered to her to have her hair and her make-up, and whatever else she dreamt of, done, but Maria had snatched up the opportunity. Sunny, however, was au naturel, the way she always was, and she refused to change herself to fit, to seek to embrace some perfected specimen of herself to try and copy the same quality as La Bambina, because that would be a no hopers' game. She couldn't do it. She wasn't classically beautiful or perfectly built in that tall, slender way to show off the latest fashions.

And then, with all that very much in her mind, Raj came to her and said, 'You look amazing in that outfit.'

Sunny almost laughed because it was so ridiculous a comment in such company. 'Thanks,' she said politely.

Raj thought it was an unexpectedly gorgeous dress, but then, it really didn't matter what she wore when he only wanted her out of it. But there it was and at least the garment showed off her magnificent bosom The display of those peachy opulent slopes of feminine flesh turned him on. He couldn't help it with her, she was just *her*, but she dressed as if she were enormous and he had to remember that.

Idly he wondered who was responsible for that. Christabel, who had been built like a toothpick, or other relatives, who might also have enjoyed a different shape? Or the boyfriends, who hadn't appeared in the investigative report because none had been visible, past or present. Even so, Raj refused to credit that a woman with Sunny's tiny but highly desirable body shape and gorgeous face had been noticed by only him. *Of course*, there had been men, but she had been discreet with her private life, he reflected grimly, wondering why that awareness of her past should bother him, because the one thing he had never ever been with women was possessive.

Drinks were served. La Bambina hovered round Raj like a shadow, always within reach, almost slavish in her desire to please. Sunny watched as the brunette ferried drinks to him, ignoring the servers available, instead stationing herself at Raj's elbow, ever ready, it seemed, to rush and attend to his every request. And if anything, it made Sunny realise how she and Raj would never suit, even in the short term. She wasn't the type to wait on her man as if he were some god. That was a fact. Why accepting that truth distressed her, she refused to recognise. In Raj's world, women seemed worryingly lower level, catering to the big guy distinguishable by his wealth and power. But then, that was her making judgements based on slender evidence, she scolded herself.

Of course, La Bambina was one of his mistresses. What else could she be?

There were little touches that Sunny was hyper-aware of occurring between the couple. The brunette would brush his shoulder, his elbow, truly any part of him that was decently within reach, nothing jarring or too intimate but still little feminine hints that this guy belonged to her in an intimate way. Raj, however, didn't touch Bambina once, but then Sunny suspected that he was by nature an undemonstrative male.

They went into dinner in another shockingly opulent saloon and the dishes were out-of-this-world tasty but Sunny was pushed to eat a few mouthfuls, in spite of her healthy appetite. Beside her, Maria was agog, drinking in every aspect of her surroundings, and Raj rose in her estimation by not having barred the nanny, a paid employee, from the meal. Even so, Sunny found that she couldn't take her attention off Raj, accepting little titbits La Bambina passed him as if they were lovers of long-standing familiarity. And obviously they *were*…

'I thought you would enjoy this…' Raj announced over the coffee when they had all moved into another reception area and he reached for her as though she were his partner, hand on her elbow to bring her up out of her seat and forward, which won her a huge disconcerted glance from La Bambina, which she might have enjoyed in any other mood because the brunette had pretty much ignored both her and the nanny, concentrating her energies and her chatter purely on Raj.

It was a Monet, one of the waterlily series and, of course, as an artist, Sunny had noticed it the moment they had entered, but there it hung on the wall without fanfare or any special staging, giving her merely a hint of what Raj's riches could acquire.

'It's truly amazing,' she whispered frankly, leaning in nearer than she had ever been able to get to a museum exhibit. 'Simply being able to be this close to a masterpiece is a huge thrill.'

His black brows lifted in surprise. 'You don't show that.'

'My appreciation is expressed quietly,' she murmured softly.

'I have another painting onboard that you would like,' he began, but La Bambina appeared beside them and started to gush about the Monet, reeling off all the facts that any amateur art enthusiast might have shared, not all accurate either, but Sunny made no comment, smiling politely and curling her nails into her palms until they bit like talons. It was an unfamiliar feeling for her.

She felt sick with jealousy and it horrified her. After all, even Jack, married at twenty-one with a baby proudly on the way, had not inspired her with that sin. That development had not been unexpected. Jack might have loved her but love hadn't been enough. Jack had decided that he wanted kids, above all, and her impairment had ensured that he went after that goal like a bullet out of a gun. It was a cause of rather bitter amusement that Raj would want a fertile lover about as much as he would want a needy, demanding woman in his bed. Raj had no idea of sharing a future or a life with her, and her feelings of jealousy, inspired by his gorgeous side-kick, Bambina, were foolish, because she very much doubted that he saw the brunette as much more important to him.

Maria was sharing her cabin with Pansy and had been dismayed when Sunny had suggested they swop accommodation, anxiously pointing out that she had been hired to look after Sunny's niece and needed to do her job. Sunny returned to her cabin alone, changed into a cool cotton slip of a nightdress and donned her robe. Then she paced restlessly, attention falling on the call button she had been urged to use to request service, only she didn't think using it after midnight would be very considerate of the crew.

She wished she were in her studio, within reach of a way to divert her buzzing energy into something positive. Frowning, she left her cabin without further deliberation. What was the matter with her?

Yes, it had been a jarring experience to finally meet a male, who attracted her and realise that she couldn't have him. But life was full of jarring, wounding experiences, she reminded herself irritably as she walked up to the upper decks where public spaces abounded. A father who had no interest in her had been the first of hers, a sister who had never accepted her as a sister had been the next, followed by Jack and then, one by one, the deaths of everyone she loved. Pansy, she conceded, was the single most wonderful thing that had ever happened to her, so why was she pining for a male she barely knew?

'Miss Barker?' A steward appeared in the doorway of the saloon, startling her. 'Can I get you anything?'

'I'd love a cup of tea,' she said a little chokily. 'Is
it OK to go outside?'

In answer he rammed open doors leading out onto
a deck for her while reciting all the many different
teas available onboard. 'English tea,' she selected,
the slight breeze catching the dampness on her face.

The *Belanger I* wasn't sailing anywhere until she
and Pansy left for their flight home in the morning. And then it was cruising...where? Well, she had
no idea, no idea when they would see Raj again either. Possibly in a month's time? She would have to
steel herself for monthly visits but at least then she
wouldn't be struggling not to think about what he
was doing with Bambina in his bedroom as she was
thinking tonight. Her face burned, her eyes, however, stung and she dashed angrily at them as her
tea arrived on a handsome tray. Honestly, the way
she was carrying on and making a meal of her little disappointment was ridiculous. Anyone could be
forgiven for thinking that she had fallen in love with
the guy at first sight!

Blinking rapidly, she sipped her tea, fighting to
calm herself. She wasn't accustomed to dealing with
such a crazy surge of emotions and if Jack hadn't
brought them out of her, what was it that made Raj
different? And then what was her worst nightmare at
that moment happened. Raj stepped out onto the deck

to join her. Raj, more casually clad than had been his wont to date, well-worn jeans hugging his long strong thighs and slim hips, a shirt partially unbuttoned to display a slice of bronzed masculine chest.

'Raj...' she mumbled weakly, horrendously unprepared and conscious of her less than pristine appearance because she hadn't believed anyone else, other than possibly the crew, would be up and about at one in the morning.

He dropped down into an athletic crouch in front of the cushioned seat she was trying to sink into unnoticed, subjecting her to the full onslaught of those intense intelligent dark eyes of his. 'What's wrong?'

'Nothing's wrong!' she exclaimed, wincing at the defensive squeak of her reaction.

Her face was streaked with tears and he hated the fragile vulnerability he saw etched there in her evasive gaze, hated it as much as he would have hated knowing that he was responsible for her plight. When the steward had mentioned that she was up and seemed troubled, he had leapt straight out of bed. He didn't know why, didn't know why it even mattered to him, because she and whatever might be upsetting her were none of his business.

He leant forward and with his thumb rubbed away a tear still wet on her cheekbone. 'You've been crying. I wouldn't be a good host if I didn't ask why.'

'You're a very good host, Raj. I'm just up here having my own little personal pity party and thank you, but there's nothing anyone can do to help.'

Raj vaulted upright again and dropped down into the seat beside her. 'I don't believe that.'

'Won't Bambina be looking for you?' Sunny asked quietly, trying to make the question sound casual. 'It's the middle of the night.'

His level black brows drew together. 'Why would she be looking for me in the middle of the night?' He paused and then he just as suddenly barked out a laugh. 'You can't have thought… *Bambina?*' he gasped. 'Me with her? Are you joking? She'd be a stage five clinger if I opened my bedroom door!'

The shock of that unchoreographed and utterly unexpected statement of denial sank through Sunny like a shock wave and did nothing immediate to fix her anxious mood. 'But, I mean, I thought you were…together.'

'Never,' Raj declared bluntly. 'She often acts as my hostess when I'm in Italy. That is why she was on board this evening. I thought you would feel safer.'

'Safer?' Sunny stressed in bewilderment. 'Why would I have needed her here to feel safer?'

Now it was Raj's turn to study her in confusion. 'Once I'd made my interest clear and you had said no, I believed you would feel nervous of spending the night on my yacht without another woman around.'

'Like a *ch-ch-chaperone*?' Sunny stammered with difficulty while the most colossal giggle built and built inside her tight chest. 'But Maria is here.'

'Staff don't count the same way,' he pointed out,

watching her face grow pink and taut and her lift a hand up to cram it against her soft pink lips.

Sunny went into a choking burst of coughing and turned her head away and down. No, she couldn't laugh and risk offending him when he had taken every precaution possible to ensure that she felt *safe* with him. 'Raj…I feel safe with you even after saying no,' she framed unevenly. 'I don't think you would do anything I didn't want you to do.'

'Good to know,' he murmured drily. 'But you still haven't told me why you were crying. I'm probably not the best person around for a therapy session but it seems like I'm the only one available right now.'

Sunny snatched in a deep breath. 'I was thinking about the people in my life who aren't here any more and feeling sad. Sometimes I do that and have a wallow but it's no reason for anyone else to worry about me.'

'But *I* don't like you feeling sad,' Raj told her levelly.

'I'll try never to do it around you again,' she swore on the edge of another inappropriate giggle, all desire to cry fully quenched now.

'Who do you miss the most?' he asked quietly.

'Mum,' she admitted tightly, her eyes dismaying her with a sudden prickle of more impending moisture, making her blink. 'She walked back late from a friend's one evening and got hit by a car. It was so sudden. She was like a bright light in our lives and then she was just…*gone*. My grandmother was devastated. She didn't expect her daughter to pass before she did. A lot of people loved her even if my father didn't.'

Sunny was disconcerted as a pair of hands slid beneath her slumped body and scooped her up and onto Raj's lap and she turned questioning violet eyes up to Raj.

'You were crying again and I'm trying to comfort you. Don't expect me to be good at it. I don't know how,' he concluded bluntly.

Her hand came up to cradle one side of his lean, darkly handsome face, small fingers stroking his stubbled jawline in a soothing motion. 'But you're trying and that's what counts.'

'Does it?' he breathed unconvinced, instinctively leaning his jaw into her soft palm and rubbing it.

And Sunny didn't even think about it, she just stretched up and kissed him, not an ardent kiss, merely a soothing brush of lips. Raj, however, had a different intent. The tip of his tongue snaked out to stab her lips apart and gain access and, within seconds, soothing turned into volatile and passionate. A little gasp sounded low in her throat as her head spun with the intoxication of that close contact with him. Her whole body felt as though it were lighting up with euphoria and her heart was hammering so hard, it seemed to be racing through her very veins.

'Is this a yes or a no?' Raj rumbled against her, sounding very much like a grizzly bear struggling with speech.

It was a moment of truth, voiced, perhaps unfortunately, when Sunny's blissed-out gaze was welded to intense dark eyes that glowed bronze, and her hands rose of their own volition to rest on his big shoulders as if to steady herself in an unsafe world. 'I can't think when you kiss me,' she objected.

'Either you want to have sex with me…or you don't,' Raj breathed, clearly out of patience, of which she suspected he had very little.

But something in that blunt, impatient declaration made Sunny smile and laugh, absolute certainty rippling through her in that same moment. Yes, it was a big step to decide to have sex for the very first time, but she also felt that it was past time she stopped walling herself off from ordinary life because Jack had let her down. His life had moved on but hers had in many ways stayed static and that shamed her pride in her own strength of mind. The right guy just hadn't come along, or possibly she had not been ready to recognise him, but Raj was different, Raj with his banked-down intensity, restless energy and his wonderful way of looking at her as though she were the only woman in the world.

'Yes,' she murmured tautly. 'My answer is yes but, bearing in mind your lifestyle, it can only ever be *one* night.'

Long fingers tugged up her chin, intense dark eyes assailing hers. 'Why?'

'Because that is the only thing that makes sense for

us. We'll get this crazy attraction out of our systems and go back to normal,' she told him with determination.

'I'm not sure I work that way.'

'I think you'll find out that I was just a crazy notion.'

A reluctant laugh was wrenched from him. 'But why would you want to think that of yourself?'

'I could be wrong but I doubt it.'

Speech fled as he crushed her parted lips hungrily beneath his again and pounding excitement infiltrated her as well.

The excitement was new to her, refreshingly, shockingly new, and it seemed to sweep away everything else. She knew that there were other women in the background of his life, but she didn't think she needed to concern herself with that reality if he and she were to be together only one night and never again. She could make her peace with that decision, accepting that it was an imperfect solution but that it was the best she could come up with that allowed both of them to continue leading their own lives as they wanted.

Raj sprang upright, still holding her in his arms. 'You're a continual surprise to me.'

'You should put me down.'

'Why? I like carrying you,' Raj confided, gazing down at her with avid dark eyes as he stalked across the reception area and up steps. 'Maybe I'm scared you'll run away.'

'I'm not an inconsistent woman.'

'You've changed your mind twice today and it could happen again. Of course, you are free to change your mind at any time,' he assured her with studious gravity.

'I unnerve you,' Sunny guessed in dismay.

Raj's sensual lips compressed. 'There's just a tiny touch of chaos about you. It's unnerving but it's also fascinating…in an odd way.'

They were inside a very large, dimly lit bedroom. The night skies were visible through the glass roof high above. He settled her down with care on the rumpled bed and hit a button to send a cover over the roof above, sealing them into greater darkness and privacy.

'I should warn you,' Sunny said, pushing herself up on her elbows, 'I haven't done this before. I'm a virgin.'

His black brows pleated in unconcealed surprise.

'Sorry about that,' she mumbled in the silence that stretched.

Raj frowned uneasily. 'You're as rare as a unicorn and I'm a man who enjoys rarity. But I can't understand why you would still be that innocent.'

'I was just never tempted enough to get into it physically with anyone…until you.'

'But I'm not offering you a relationship.'

'I'm not looking for one. Oh, is that what's worrying you? That I might not know what I'm doing? Or that I might attach expectations to you afterwards?' Sunny smiled with rueful amusement. 'Trust me. I know what I'm doing and I'm not in a place where I could have a relationship either.'

The tension in his lean strong face evaporated, his misgivings about becoming her first lover quelled.

And Sunny laughed as he came down to her, long fingers tracing her cheekbones, his eyes brilliant with hunger, a predatory smile curving his shapely mouth. He lifted her back into his arms and kissed her senseless. A stirring heat awakened in her pelvis and her nipples prickled and tightened. He leant back to slide her out of her robe and yanked his shirt off over his head with one hand in an easy movement.

Looking at him, she felt her mouth run dry. He was all solid muscle sheathed in sleek olive skin, a muscled six-pack and the fabled vee carving down to his hips coming into view as he stood up to unbutton his jeans. His attraction was visceral in its masculinity. Black hair tousled, he returned to her and pulled her back to him, framing her face with his big hands, ravishing her soft lips with raw passion before laying her back against the pillows.

'I want to fall on you like a starving wolf,' he growled, tugging at the nightdress that still shielded her from him and extracting her from it with determination. 'That's how ravenous you make me.'

He bent his head over the lush curve of her breasts, hands rising to cup her plump flesh, mouth darting down to tug insistently at the swollen tips. Her fingers came down on his wide shoulders, delved into his thick black hair as she twisted, breathless, at the sweet surge of response arrowing up between her legs. Little sounds escaped her and self-consciousness never came to claim her because she had never wanted anything in that moment as much as she wanted Raj. It was intimate and sensual, two things she had never allowed herself to experience, and what she was feeling now when he touched her was overwhelming.

Slowly he worked his path down over her shapely curves, lingering wherever he wished. He discovered with an appreciative laugh how she reacted when he kissed the pulse in her neck and plucked at the tender skin there with the edge of his teeth. Her hips writhed as he concentrated on the damp pink lips between her thighs. She learned minute by minute to want more, indeed to want more so fiercely that she had to resist the temptation to try and persuade him to go faster.

He traced her with long skilled fingers that made her tremble. He circled her clitoris with the most terrifying restrained delicacy and then lowered his head there to explore her with his mouth and his tongue until she was thrashing and squirming in a feverish delirium of arousal. The slow, agonising build-up to that level of excitement was almost more than she could bear. Her back arched and her lips opened on a gasp as the waves of sensation drove her up to a height and pushed her over it into a shattering climax.

Wrung out in the aftermath, Sunny gazed up at him with a heart that was still pounding and a body that was still singing.

'And now for the main event,' Raj teased with a dark edge to his deep voice, rearranging her with sure hands when she was certain that she was so relaxed she would flop if he freed her. Protection, he reminded himself, marvelling that he had almost overlooked that necessity and then recalling that Sunny couldn't get pregnant and throwing the idea of precautions to the four winds.

'Just get it over with,' Sunny whispered ruefully, because she had never ever expected much from her first experience of sex.

'Wrong mindset.' Raj slid between her parted thighs and nudged his hard, velvety length against her tender entrance. 'It will be better than that.

'You don't know but you *should*. We're dynamite together,' Raj continued with blazing confidence as he shifted his lean hips and slowly eased into her.

Raj gazed down at her with immense satisfaction because he already felt as though he had waited for her...*for ever*. She lifted his day, she brightened his often gloomy horizon, and of course she was saying all that stuff about one night only but he didn't believe a word of it. She played safe, she *always* played safe. He had recognised that in her at their very first meeting. Sunny kept herself safe from change by living in her little cocoon of rural anonymity and he threatened all that with his alternative outlook.

Sunny shimmied her hips a little in invitation as she felt him invade her all too eager body. A quiver travelled up her spine before dispelling into other more sensitive places, anticipation rising in a swooshing tide of hunger. He lifted her legs and spread her wider, seated himself deeper and pushed and there was a brief, bearable sting of pain that made her brow furrow as she waited for worse to come, but it didn't come. That was that, that little pang of discomfort, and all her worst expectations had failed to pan out.

Raj emitted a stifled groan. 'You're so tight…and you feel so good.'

Relieved of her concern, Sunny shifted up into the glorious heat and weight of him, finally surrendering to the experience, and all resistance fled as he sank harder and faster into the liquid heat of her. Excitement curled at the heart of her, sensation spreading out in a slow, breathtaking ripple that engulfed her body and her senses. He was stretching her, holding her and all those feelings seemed to coalesce in a starburst of intense emotion and feeling that stoked the heat at her core. As he took her with increasingly relentless strokes, all thought ceased and she became a creature of reaction instead. And her response climbed and climbed to magnificent heights before he pushed her over the peak a second time and the drowning sweet pleasure took over again.

'We're amazing together,' Raj husked, rolling over and still retaining a grip on her to tug her into a cooler stretch of the bed.

Sunny stilled for a brief moment but she had heard

how it went on a one-night stand and from what she had understood a woman should not hang around afterwards. She pulled away. 'I'll get going now,' she said flatly.

'I want you to stay,' Raj decreed.

'But there's a sort of etiquette to these occasions… I understand,' she told him anxiously. 'Staying on isn't the thing.'

Raj shifted across the bed and closed both arms round her. 'I don't want you to leave.'

Sunny was surprised and Raj was even more surprised when those words escaped him, he who always slept alone, who hated women who tried to linger. But somehow Sunny put him in pursuit mode and that was an entirely new experience for him. Was she being elusive as part of a deliberate act? As that cynical suspicion filtered in, he flipped over to lean over her and met wide, troubled eyes, empty of any calculation other than the fastest route to the exit.

'Raj…I—'

'Stay,' he told her with emphasis.

Sunny froze, only losing her tension when he reached for her again. 'I'm not used to this,' she admitted awkwardly.

Raj loosened his hold on her. 'Relax with me,' he suggested.

'I can't… I'm not used to sharing this kind of intimacy,' she muttered unhappily. 'What if Pansy needs me during the night?'

Raj reached for the phone and spoke into it. 'There. You can be reached now.'

'You mean…you actually told people that I'm here with *you*?' Sunny gasped in horror. 'Where's your discretion?'

'You killed it. Go to sleep,' he urged.

And somehow, she did, yielding to the exhaustion of travel and unexpected events and more emotions than she knew how to handle. She drifted off, only to waken at some timeless stage of the night with Raj asking her if it was all right.

'What's all right?'

'Sex without protection,' he framed in an urgent undertone. 'I'm tested every month and I haven't been with anyone since we met. You said you can't get pregnant, so…? I've never had unprotected sex.'

'Go ahead,' she whispered, shimmying her hips back to his and his arousal with sensual pleasure.

And he did and it was slow and astonishingly exciting as his hands glided over her with wondrous expertise, tantalising and arousing until her head was falling back and she was in a paradise of intense sensation and then he was there exactly where she needed him to be. Hard and urgent and demanding and by the time he finished she was drifting off to sleep again, utterly ignoring his suggestion that she join him in the shower. A step too far, she was tempted to tell him, but she felt way too lazy and still too inhibited to subject herself to that test. Tomorrow was a new day, a moving-on day, she reminded herself doggedly, wondering why Raj wasn't acting as standoffish in the aftermath as she had naïvely expected.

CHAPTER FIVE

RAJ WAKENED LATER than was his wont, in an empty bed, and he immediately frowned.

Why had Sunny not wakened him? Most particularly after they had shared such an astonishing night together. Had he been the sort of guy who suffered from a fragile ego, he could have felt slighted. But there was nothing fragile about Raj's ego, particularly when he was recalling a sleepless night of passion such as he had never before enjoyed. She had wanted him as much as he had wanted her, he reflected with confidence as he strode into the shower. But even so, he was already recalling those admittedly glorious moments of unprotected sex and tensing over them. He had got carried away. He would address that potential problem before she flew back to the UK.

Of course, Sunny had got up early to be available for their niece, he assumed, content to forgive her on that score alone. A child's needs *should* take precedence over the adults' desires. He could only wish that he had enjoyed the nurture of a mother like that. Unfortunately, fate had cursed him with a weak, cowardly mother, one enthralled for years by a cruel, manipulative man. Only Clara's second pregnancy had inspired and strengthened her enough to walk out on Raj's father. Pansy, however, would only ever enjoy the blessing of Sunny and all the love and attention Sunny could shower on the child.

In her cabin, Sunny finished packing her overnight bag, having already attended to Pansy's. Every too quick movement jarred her still tender body with muscular aches and faint little pangs in parts never before used with such thoroughness. She smiled to herself. It had been one magical, unforgettable night, she savoured, grateful that she had had the courage to take up the opportunity rather than remaining controlled by a better-buried past. There would be an aftermath of sadness eventually for what could *not* be in the future, she conceded ruefully, but then that was life, always giving with one hand and then taking with the other. In the meantime, it was only human to be wondering if it was normal to make love that many times in the space of a few hours. Raj had been…insatiable. There was no other word for his hunger for her and she had felt empowered by her apparent desirability. Only that was a shallow, superficial thing, she acknowledged, shamefaced, and not something she could reasonably feel proud of attracting.

As a crew member came to collect their luggage, she was informed that Raj had asked to see her in his office. Leaving Pansy with Maria, who was planning to take the child out onto the deck to see the school of dolphin whose presence they had been alerted to by the attendant, Sunny followed the same man into a lift that whisked her up to the top deck. Her cheeks were hot at the prospect of seeing Raj again. Tiptoeing out of his cabin at dawn had been an easy escape but one that now had to be paid for with the awkward first meeting she had earlier ducked.

'Good morning, Sunny,' Raj greeted her with an expansive smile of welcome. 'I expected to have breakfast with you and Pansy, but you sneaked off early without rousing me.'

Raj looked magnificent in a pale linen suit, more casual in cut than she was accustomed to seeing on him, although nothing could diminish his height and breadth or the taut, fit definition of his musculature below the dark blue open-necked shirt he sported. That very thought made her face warm again and fired an uneasy clenching sensation low in her pelvis, making her shift in her seat.

'I thought it was easier for us both my way,' she confided unevenly, breathing challenged by his proximity as he directed her down into a comfortable armchair graced with a panoramic view of the Italian coast and the sea. A faint hint of his designer cologne flared her nostrils and made her even stiffer. 'You've got the most amazing office environment to enjoy up here.'

A knock sounded on the door and a tray arrived.

'Soothing camomile tea,' Raj announced, dark eyes gleaming with amusement.

'And coffee for you. The tea would have been a healthier option but just ignore me when I preach,' she told him.

'We were rather bold last night,' Raj remarked. 'I sincerely hope that there isn't any chance of a child coming from that boldness.'

Sunny froze. 'None whatsoever. I'm infertile,' she assured him, pale as a ghost at having to repeat what was soothing news to him but a painful recollection for her.

Raj relaxed his guard. 'I would like you to extend your stay onboard,' he stated with the utmost casualness.

Dismay lit Sunny's strained eyes and she lowered her lashes. 'I'm afraid I can't. I have to get back to my studio and my animals.'

'I can fix all that,' Raj pointed out, smooth as ice, bronzed eyes wandering over her at his leisure, his gaze heating her up wherever it lingered, swelling her breasts inside her bra, creating a damp heat between her thighs, which she pressed together hard. 'I'll have your art supplies flown out or new supplies obtained. I will organise care for your livestock. You won't need to worry about anything.'

Sunny breathed in slow and deep. 'But I *want* to go home,' she said tightly. 'I've really enjoyed this very glamorous trip and your hospitality. It's been a treat and I mean that. I'm very grateful.'

'Did the sex qualify as a treat or merely as an aspect of my hospitality?' Raj derided.

Sunny paled at his tone and the tension that had hardened his lean, darkly handsome features to granite. 'That's not a fair comment. We both knew and accepted what last night was.'

'I know what you said but I didn't believe you or accept what you said or even agree with it,' Raj admitted boldly.

'Oh, dear,' Sunny mumbled uneasily. Shaken by that unvarnished warning of intent, she slowly sipped her tea in its bone china monogrammed cup, the saucer rattling a little as her hand trembled. 'You should've said all that to me last night.'

'What guy would when he wants a woman? I didn't believe you meant it because your decision doesn't make any sense.'

'It makes *perfect* sense,' Sunny sliced in a little louder, determined to be heard. 'We have different values, different lifestyles. One night was self-indulgent but comparatively harmless in the long term. It ended it, no hard feelings.'

'Newsflash…I've got hard feelings!' Raj shot back at her rawly.

'There's nothing I can do about that except wish that I hadn't made the decision to stay with you last night,' Sunny replied curtly. 'It's not as if it's a rejection. It's simply rational and practical. And we shouldn't be confusing this relationship for Pansy's benefit. We're her uncle and her aunt. We are not lovers.'

'That's not a matter of concern while she is still so young!' Raj interposed fiercely. 'I wanted you last night. I want you now. I'm not a changeable individual. You cannot switch off a response like that, and that you believe you can only proves how out of your depth you are!'

'I didn't say it would be *easy* to switch off again,' Sunny objected as she set down the tea and stood up, feeling intimidated by the fact that he was still standing. 'But that's the price for the freedom we enjoyed last night. If we continued some sort of affair, it would get messy. You wouldn't like messy and I refuse to break my own rules.'

'You're not a teenager with a curfew any more, Sunny,' Raj said very drily. 'You can make your own rules.'

'Not about accepting your other women, not about the basic truth that we couldn't work in any field because we are so different,' she protested and then she paused, and, recognising the shielded detachment in his cool bronzed gaze, she suddenly threw up her hands in frustration. 'Oh, why am I even bothering trying to explain when you're not listening…? Just as you *refused* to listen to me last night. If you don't want to hear something, you ignore it. If you don't like it, you ignore it. Well, maybe that works in your world and people feel forced to accept your point of view as supreme, but it doesn't work in mine and it never will!'

'Have you anything else to say?' Raj enquired glacially. 'Or are you done shouting at me?'

'I was not shouting!' Sunny fired back at him furiously.

'You are definitely shouting,' Raj informed her gently, watching her pace in front of him, another one of her all-enveloping shapeless dresses flapping around her ankles. 'And I have a very low tolerance for being shouted at.'

'Oh, shut up!' Sunny loosed at him in ferocious annoyance at that measured declaration. 'Nobody has ever got me as mad as you get me! You stand there giving forth like Moses off the Mount but you're not going to get away with doing it to me!'

'And I won't allow you to sidle away from the truth,' Raj countered, stepping between her and the door. 'Is that how you work, Sunny? All charm and appeal until someone dares to challenge you? And then, you *run away*? That's not how I work.'

'You're being difficult,' Sunny protested.

'But isn't that what you expected from me?' Raj tossed back, still acting as a very effective block between her and the exit. 'I won't allow you to run away from what you refuse to face.'

'I don't refuse to face anything!' Sunny flung at him angrily.

'I'm sorry but you *do*,' Raj countered with grave intent. 'You don't want this attraction because it doesn't meet your requirements…whatever they may be!'

'Like mistresses in every port of call…like *that's* normal!' Sunny exclaimed in a total fury exceeding anything she had ever felt before. She was outraged that Raj was daring to behave as though he were a single guy able to be with her alone. 'Yeah, sorry about those normal requirements of mine, but actually they're fairly basic…if you *can* tune into the regular expectations of the average woman, which I'm not sure you can.'

Raj stalked forward a step. 'And what are those expectations?'

'The expectations you're determined not to hear,' Sunny slung back at him vehemently. 'I don't *share*! Would you agree to share me with another man?'

A muscle pulled tight at the corner of his unsmiling mouth. 'Of course not.'

'There you are, then,' Sunny said softly, the anger leaving her in a relieving surge as she realised that she had finally found an argument that he respected. 'You're looking at what you offered me and you wouldn't accept that for yourself. Is that sexism? Hypocrisy? I don't know. What I *do* know is that I won't accept *less* than you evidently would.'

Raj gritted his even white teeth. He wasn't accustomed to being outdone in a dispute but he could not, at that moment, come up with a reasonable response and that infuriated him. He was neither sexist, nor hypocritical. The world he lived in had taught him to adapt to certain unavoidable changes. He wanted sex like any young, healthy male but if he didn't want his bedroom exploits and secrets spread across the tabloids for public consumption, he had to take specific steps to protect himself. And that had inevitably led to the mistress solution, women who accepted that sex was basically all that he required from them. Only Sunny did not fit into that category.

'I understand that this is a negotiation,' he returned levelly.

Sunny stared back at him in shock at that assurance. 'That's *not* what this is.'

'What else can it be? You tell me what you will not accept. I may or may not choose to meet your terms.'

'You've been in business for far too long,' Sunny argued unhappily. 'Relationships do not fall into the business realm.'

Raj gave her a very wry smile, lips turning up at the corner in acknowledgement of their directly opposed viewpoints. 'Sunny…' he murmured gently. 'I have never *been* in a relationship with a woman.'

Sunny was aghast. 'But that's not possible.'

'It is perfectly possible in my sphere. The women… it is only physical. There is no relationship. Barely any conversation…' His smile became pained. 'Then again, I am a male with few words and sharing my thoughts feels unnatural. They give me sex. I give them a comfortable lifestyle. It is an exchange at the most basic level and nothing more.'

And it was one of those odd moments that she experienced with Raj when she wanted to wrap her arms round him and point out that he never stopped talking with her. Only then did it occur to her that he had already had something different with her from what he had had with others of her sex and her heart still gave a painful tug. 'Raj,' she sighed helplessly.

'It's much more with you.'

'Yes, I get that,' she muttered, suddenly thrown on the back foot again, unable to see how they could possibly go in that direction.

'Last night…was special,' Raj volunteered as she came into his radius on her wandering path to the door. 'You are the first woman I have trusted in many years. I had unprotected sex with you. I have never before even contemplated taking such a risk with a woman but you are different. You…I trust.'

'Yes,' she whispered shakily, overwhelmed by that claim, secretly delighted by it.

'You, I want,' Raj completed, reaching out to close his big hands gently over her arms and draw her close.

The scent of him was like an aphrodisiac in the air as Sunny drew it in. She had spent the night in his arms, a night such as she had never dreamt of having, and every moment of it had been precious to her. For the very first time that morning, she relaxed, drawn by the heat and reassuring solidity of his lean, powerful physique.

'And you want me too,' Raj completed tautly.

'But I want more of you than you're willing to give,' Sunny chimed in helplessly.

Raj lifted her up to him and crushed her parted

lips beneath his and she could feel her own body thrum and pulse like an engine suddenly switched on. Her head fell back as he sent his tongue delving between her readily parted lips to explore further. A quiver of hunger rippled through her and, that fast, she wanted him again and it was an inexpressible need in the situation they were in. Shaken by the experience, torn in two by it, she pulled herself back and stepped away, her lovely face flushed and troubled.

'We can't do this. I should go and be with Pansy.'

'Your mind is closed to me, closed to any solution that does not agree with yours.'

'That is as may be, Raj…but I'm free to have my own opinion and protect myself.'

His brilliant dark eyes rested on her and hardened. 'Of course, but you insult me when you imply that I would harm you in any way.'

A rueful smile curved Sunny's reddened mouth. 'You wouldn't do it deliberately, but you don't look at the whole picture and you would do it without intending to,' she responded quietly.

And she accompanied him down onto the deck where Pansy was racing about in pursuit of an electronic cat that purred and made squeaky noises.

'I don't give her advanced toys of that sort,' Sunny confided. 'I prefer the basic stuff.'

'Don't restrict her to what you played with as a child,' Raj advised. 'The world has moved on, as must we to stay relevant.'

* * *

On the flight back home on the private jet, Sunny was exhausted. Pansy slumbered beside her and, eventually, Sunny drifted off as well. After all, she hadn't slept much the previous night and she was emotionally drained in a way she had never experienced before. Raj wound her up and more feelings than she had known she even possessed came surging up out of her to create an inner turmoil that scared her.

The first thing she noticed when she drove into the yard was that her barn had been repaired. How could that be possible? She climbed out and released Pansy before standing back to get a proper look at the barn. Before she'd left, she had only reached the stage of requesting quotes from local builders. Unfortunately, the insurance company had already indicated that they were not prepared to pay for the whole job because the barn rafters were rotten. Since she was still recovering from the recent stresses of the court case on her bank account, she had planned to go for the best repair job she could afford and hope the building came through the winter intact. But now her barn rejoiced in what appeared to be a completely new roof.

'What happened to the barn?' she asked her friend, Gemma, as she carted sundry bags into the hall.

Gemma was her nearest neighbour and the older woman fostered many rescue animals. All Sunny's pets had come to her through Gemma and when either of them travelled, they looked after the other's home and the animals as well.

'The barn?' Gemma's pencilled brows disappeared behind her auburn fringe. 'I never saw a team of men work as hard in my life as they did. They arrived almost as soon as you left and they had the old roof off and the new one on by this morning. They worked all night with floodlights and the like. Muffy spent the night in the paddock and I took the pets home with me. Oh, by the way…'

A chihuahua raced forward and gambolled at her feet in welcome.

'Bert's been returned.'

'So I can see. What went wrong for him this time?' Sunny asked, stooping down to pet the little animal while her brain was still turning over 'team', 'worked all night' and 'floodlights'. Unless she was very much mistaken, only Raj could command such astonishing service.

'Bert barked through the fence at his new owner's neighbour's dog and wouldn't stop, so back he came. He's his own worst enemy.' Gemma sighed. 'But he's been very quiet since he came back through the door. He hasn't annoyed Bear once. Oh, yes, to keep you up to date with local gossip…apparently, Jack Henderson's marriage blew up last week.'

The sudden change of topic bemused Sunny. 'My goodness…what happened?'

'Nobody knows exactly. Ellie Henderson has moved out of the marital home and in with Jack's cousin, but she's left the kids behind with Jack. His mother is living with him now to help with the grand-kids.'

'Wow.' Sunny was taken aback.

'Didn't you and Jack once date?' Gemma prompted.

'When we were teenagers, we were close, but we broke up and never really talked after that,' she con-fided.

Bear lay down at Pansy's feet and the little girl giggled, bending down to stroke his broad back. Sunny made tea for Gemma and chatted and the whole time her brain was working at a mile a minute on how best to tackle the barn problem with Raj. As soon as her friend had left, Sunny lifted her phone and rang Raj.

'Did you arrange for my barn to be fixed?' she asked.

'Yes. I own construction companies.'

'And did you arrange for the work to be done while I was in Italy?' Sunny asked tightly.

'Of course I did,' Raj confirmed without a shade of embarrassment or remorse. 'It meant that you wouldn't have your life disrupted.'

'And it also meant that I wouldn't be here to ob-ject to the work being done,' she slotted in curtly.

'Obviously,' Raj agreed. 'I didn't want you to make a fuss.'

Sunny gritted her teeth. 'Send me the bill.'

'Oh, no, I won't be doing that,' Raj declared. 'You

sent me a valuable painting which cost me nothing. I'm saying thank you with a new roof on your barn.'

Sunny dragged in a steadying breath. 'You know that that painting was a gift and, besides, you already sent me a scratching post for my cat.'

'Only because I was hoping you would take the log out of your living room. You're family, Sunny. You needed the barn fixed and I took care of it. That's what I do. Now I can sleep at night knowing that Muffy is dry and warm.'

Sunny swore under her breath. 'Raj, I *can't*.'

'Could we continue this some other time?' Raj enquired gently. 'I'm in the middle of a business meeting.'

'Yes, of course,' she said stiltedly and cut the call.

He was so devious and so smooth about his manipulation that he made her want to scream. And yet at heart she was grateful that the barn was no longer a problem. Worrying about how she could afford to fix it without taking out a loan had been stressful. Even trying to find builders to make a quote had been stressful. Raj had done her a favour, done Muffy a favour too, she conceded with a groan.

She texted him and attached a photo of Muffy in her stall.

Thank you very much.

That Sunday, she was picking up Pansy from the creche after the church service when she ran into Jack picking up his children from their Sunday

School classes. There was one of those uncomfortable standoffs until he smiled down at Pansy and asked with curiosity, 'And who is this?'

'My half-sister's little girl. Christabel and her husband died in an accident. I'm adopting Pansy.'

'I'm sorry for your loss…but that's wonderful news for you,' Jack said heartily.

And she looked at him: the young man who had broken her heart as a girl with his rejection. He was tall, broad and blond with frank blue eyes. The years that had passed hadn't dimmed his looks but he no longer made her heart beat a little faster. Raj had surpassed him.

In any case, she now felt sorry for Jack. His wife had been carrying on an affair with his wealthier cousin for several years. All too many people had seen Jack's wife and cousin entangled in parked cars at deserted spots. Jack had wed in haste and ensured that his wife produced four kids in swift succession, but Ellie's attention had strayed and now he was being left to raise the kids he had wanted so badly on his own. She hoped his life would smooth out again and that his children would survive the breakdown of their parents' marriage without too much damage. But her interest was no more personal than that.

Six weeks later, Sunny returned to her doctor's surgery for the results she had been promised.

She had felt out of sorts for several weeks, had felt nauseous, dizzy and off her food and, when that had escalated into actual bouts of sickness, she had gone to her doctor for a check-up. It was obvious to her that some virus had got a hold of her and she was under par, possibly in need of some kind of tonic to help her shake off the bug.

'You are pregnant,' Dr Smyth informed her quietly.

Shock engulfed Sunny in a dizzy wave of disbelief. 'But I was told that wasn't possible when I was seventeen and I've always believed that I would be childless,' she admitted.

'I don't presume to criticise the doctor who told you that.'

'No, it was actually my mother who told me that I would never have a child,' Sunny interrupted, wanting to be fair.

'You were only twelve when you had surgery after a ruptured appendix. Your reproductive organs were damaged but you were fortunate to have a skilled surgeon in the aftermath,' the older man explained. 'Evidently, the repairs he undertook and the healing that took place in your young and healthy body were successful. And here you are now...'

'Yes,' Sunny agreed, wrenched between delight and horror at the truth that she was receiving. What she had assumed was impossible was, after all, possible. And the news shook her inside out and upside down.

Good grief, how could she ever tell Raj? She had assured him that it was safe to have sex without precautions and she had been wrong. Miraculously, she had conceived, but she was not naïve enough to assume that Raj would react to her announcement in the same way. Raj would be appalled and her heart sank at the prospect of telling him…

CHAPTER SIX

SUNNY SHIFTED POSITION in the opulent limousine on the drive to Ashton Hall while absently wondering why Raj's staff had warned her to bring her passport, because they were not on this occasion leaving England.

Pansy was dozing, replete after her lunch before their departure. Maria was playing some game on her phone. She had been in the limo when it arrived to collect them, and Sunny couldn't help but be impressed by the fact that Raj had recognised that continuity of care was important for their niece's stability. Particularly, she reflected anxiously, when their every meeting with Raj seemed to happen at a different place. It had been six weeks since they had been together on his yacht, six weeks since they had talked face-to-face.

But none of that mattered now, none of the differences, none of the disagreements, she reminded herself firmly. Time had moved on for them both. Raj had his life with his other women and she had her life with Pansy and a future baby. Utterly detached, those lifestyles, she acknowledged. But...a *baby*, a joy that she had believed would never be hers, and Raj had given her that baby. Unknowingly, without intent, she conceded, that daring rush of joy draining away again into guilt and shame. Raj would never have given her that baby by intent and that truth mattered *so* much.

The limousine turned down a long leafy lane and pulled off onto a gravelled frontage to align with a jewel of a Georgian country property.

'Oh, wow!' the nanny gasped in delight. 'Working for Mr Belanger is so exciting!'

Sunny scanned the opulent vehicles already parked and the helicopters on the front lawn and thought instead that Raj was exceptionally busy. And hadn't she known that already when his staff had had to cancel his visit a fortnight earlier and remake it? Raj worked and travelled and that was his chosen way of living, because nobody could say that he worked simply to earn when he already had more money than he could use in a dozen lifetimes. No, Raj moved on to the next challenge in the science and development field, always ahead of the crowd. He used his brilliance, kept himself gainfully occupied in the world of profit and expansion, probably as he had been taught as a child, and he continually prospered and triumphed. So, why did a part of her feel sorry for Raj's inability to relax and pause to smell the roses? It was a nonsense to think that way about a male who was so phenomenally successful.

Their arrival was a repeat of their previous arrival in Italy. Staff hovered uncertainly and then Raj came striding out and Sunny's heart stopped dead and then hammered in a dangerously staccato beat because, my word, she thought in the same moment, he was beautiful. Incredibly tall, well built and superbly sophisticated, sheathed in a formal black business suit that accentuated his black hair and very dark eyes.

Pansy, unimpressed by that detachment of his, whooped and scurried forward to greet him without hesitation, reaching his knees to embrace his legs and there was the change. A smile spread across his lean, darkly handsome face like a tide and he grinned down at his niece in welcome, delighted by her enthusiasm, not yet understanding that he was the only male in Pansy's world and already undeniably special to the little girl. He scooped her up into his arms.

''Lo, Unc,' Pansy managed, a little hand reaching up to his face to touch his nose. 'Noz…eye…' she told him, keen to show off her latest learning before fumbling to a halt at his lips, forgetting that word.

'Hello, Pansy,' Raj said cheerfully. 'That's mouth… *mouth*,' he sounded out with care.

And Sunny just melted inside herself because she saw the effort he was making, the natural way he was ready and willing to interreact with their niece at the most basic level. It had only taken a little encouragement for him to stop being so self-conscious and fearful of rejection. And she could never ever air that conviction because to voice it would injure his pride. But she could see how easily he could react to having a child of his own and it hurt that she was so convinced that he would never ever offer that warmth to *their* child. An unplanned, unsought child, an accident…a *mistake*.

Raj freed Pansy as soon as she squirmed for freedom. He strode across the echoing marble hall with its chequerboard black and white floor to focus on Sunny instead. She was dressed once again in a flowing purple garment that screened all possible view of her shapely curves. And he didn't care because he now knew what lay under all that screening fabric and it was entirely his to enjoy, his to appreciate and he was, he conceded, a male very much into the concept of *his* woman only showing herself to him in private.

She was smiling, that smile lighting up her beautiful face, sunlight flooding in to gleam across the golden tumble of her hair, and he was thoroughly entranced by the prospect of the weekend ahead. Sunny…all to himself. He went hard as a rock, shifting position to accommodate that instantaneous surge of physical hunger. He felt like a teenager again. He couldn't wait, he genuinely would struggle to wait to be alone with her, finally freed from all other concerns. Just him and Sunny, just exactly as he'd planned weeks ago even if he had had to wait longer than he had hoped to see her again…

'Sunny,' he murmured softly. 'It feels like for ever since I saw you last and I'm afraid I'm about to ask you to wait yet again for me. My business conference is still current. An important person was delayed and, as a result, we are running late and my time frame has changed.'

'That's fine,' Sunny hastened to assure him as he gathered both her restive hands in his and just held them. Swoon, she was thinking dizzily, not having expected such an enthusiastic reception after their last meeting. She had been mistaken, she allowed guiltily. Clearly Raj did not hold spite. Evidently, she and Pansy got a clean sheet for every visit and that was heart-warming, particularly after what had happened between them. Instantly she relaxed on that belief, colliding with those very dark, so intense eyes of his and feeling the heat rise below her skin. He had stunning eyes and she only had to meet those eyes to remember them on her before dawn as he sank into her hard and deep and gave her the most breathtaking pleasure she had ever known.

'I've organised a tour of the house and grounds to keep you occupied and later, we're having dinner together.' With a wave of his hand, he signalled an older man. 'This is Stuart, who manages the estate here at Ashton Hall.'

'I really wasn't expecting... I mean, if you're busy, and you obviously are.'

'Right at this moment,' Raj husked, staring down at her with hungry dark eyes, 'you are the most important person.'

Sunny was stunned into silence by that announcement. Did he mean that literally? Were they at odds again in the understanding stakes? Had he assumed, because Raj was very prone to assuming stuff that suited him, that because she had fallen into his bed so easily, she would be willing to do so again? Or was she being fanciful? Imagining more than he meant? Maybe he was simply smoothing over and moving past the intimacy of that night on his yacht? Or being charming? Trying to relax her?

It was hard to tell with Raj. He wasn't like other people. He didn't always make reasonable deductions from what she saw as fact. He was quite likely to make up his own story of how he wanted things to happen inside his own complex head. And that worried her, seriously worried her because she didn't want to end up arguing with him again and increasing the tension.

But friction was inevitable, she reminded herself unhappily. She had to tell him this weekend that she was pregnant. He deserved to know that truth from the first. That wasn't something she could deny or conceal and she wanted to be fair and open with him because he would definitely prefer that approach.

Stuart showed them up an elegant staircase into bedrooms and reception areas, letting drop that all the conference visitors would be leaving and that only she and Pansy were spending the weekend. Pansy and Maria were soon ensconced in a comfortable nursery filled with new toys. Sunny was shown into a spacious bedroom where her case already awaited her. Leaving it untouched, she continued the tour with

Stuart and Pansy, walking downstairs again to admire a pillared ballroom and a gracious library and other grand reception rooms before moving outside to take in the view.

A rolling green lawn ran up to the edge of a fenced park and beyond that she could see a herd of deer grazing at the edge of dense woodland. It was peaceful and beautiful and she allowed Stuart to show her where the walled garden was before telling him that they would find their own way back. A priority for her was to let her niece enjoy a closer look at the deer.

That was achieved but the peace and quiet didn't last long because Pansy's whoops of excitement sent the herd leaping away at speed, a development that her niece found even more thrilling. After that, she headed for the walled garden where she dawdled near any promising plants with her camera and took pictures while Pansy scampered about, revelling in her freedom.

When they returned to the house, Stuart offered to have Pansy's supper brought to the nursery and she agreed. It was time to get Pansy into the bath and into her pyjamas for bed. By the time all that was accomplished, Sunny was ready to dress for dinner. When she returned to her allotted room, she found a dress hanging in a garment bag outside the wardrobe. It carried a note from Raj: 'Please wear this for me.'

Sunny frowned and extracted it from the bag. It was layered, long and stretchy and the sort of soft blue shade she liked. What on earth strange idea had

Raj taken into his handsome head? Buying a *dress* for her? And how did she refuse without causing offence? And didn't she have a big enough challenge to surmount with her unexpected pregnancy? Honey, she recalled her mother saying, was always better received than vinegar.

Showered and her usual minimal make-up applied—well, possibly rather more than usual—she donned the dress. It moulded her curves more than she liked but she appreciated the floaty upper layer and it did fit amazingly well. She might as well enjoy the sight of her waist while she still had it, she thought forlornly, because nature would soon be thickening it up. And how was Raj likely to feel about that? Well, what did that matter, considering that that night had been a one-off? Even so, nervous tension made her antsy.

Stuart knocked on the door to tell her that Raj was waiting for her downstairs.

Her heart was beating very fast when she reached the hall where Raj awaited her. He looked amazing, sleek and sophisticated in an exquisitely tailored dark suit that moulded his broad shoulders and faithfully outlined his long, powerful legs. 'We're a little late but it's a clear night for flying.'

'Flying?' she stressed in astonishment.

'Tonight, we're doing something special for dinner,' Raj informed her, walking her down the shallow steps and round the side of the house to a helicopter.

'But Pansy—'

'Maria knows that we'll be back tomorrow morning and she will be able to get in contact with us at any time,' Raj asserted. 'I've thought of everything.'

Reckoning that it was hard to combat such a claim and remain strictly polite, Sunny bundled up her skirts and began to clamber awkwardly into the helicopter, but a pair of hands settled to her hips for Raj to lift her in. Flustered, she settled in a seat and utilised the headphones she was handed. Why the heck were they doing something *special* for dinner? What was that about? Her frown deepened.

'You really are the most frustrating man I've ever met,' she told him roundly before the pilot lifted the heavy craft into the air.

Raj merely smiled. He wanted her to enjoy herself. In fact, he was determined that she should enjoy herself every moment that she was with him. He had phoned her several times over the past six weeks, ostensibly to ask after his niece, but the previous week he had noticed that Sunny seemed out of sorts, not her usual upbeat self, and it had bothered him. She needed a little fun in her life and, although he considered himself to be one of the world's most serious and least fun-loving guys, he was convinced that he could dig deep and surprise and please her.

'Paris?' she checked in wonder as the limousine powered them through the busy well-lit city streets and she peered out at the magnificent buildings. 'Just for dinner?'

'Just for dinner. I'm taking you to one of my hotels.'

'It's like being Cinderella for the night.'

'I'm no fairy godmother…nor am I a Prince Charming,' Raj proclaimed with a shudder.

A magnificent hotel dazzling with the combined light of crystal chandeliers and blazing windows awaited them. Raj swept her in through the front doors, past glittering groups of people sporting evening wear and opulent jewellery, and straight into a mirrored lift. As the doors closed on the view, she registered in horror that everyone seemed to be staring at *her*.

'Why was everyone looking at me? Do I look that strange?'

'No, of course, you don't look strange. It's my fault that people are staring,' Raj assured her in exasperation. 'The only women I'm ever seen in public with are employees. Obviously, you are not an employee and that makes you a source of interest.'

And some of the interest could be in the highly identifiable dress she wore, fresh off the catwalk and designed by the season's hottest designer, Stevie Carteret. He had seen the dress in a newspaper and had thought it looked exactly like something that Sunny would like. It was sort of floaty and enveloping but the wispy top layer was transparent and the close fit of the dress beneath showed off Sunny's glorious curves.

Sunny studied their reflection in one of the mirrors. They were the odd couple, Raj so tall, her barely reaching his chest. But even that glimpse of him, his square jawline blue black with stubble because he hadn't shaved again, his wide sculpted mouth relaxed, made her heartbeat quicken, her breath catch in her throat, that warm curling sensation of sensual familiarity spread like temptation through her pelvis.

'I'm surprised you're taking me out in public,' she confided breathlessly as he guided her out of the lift and straight across an opulent hallway into an incredibly elegant reception area.

'In today's world it's wiser to show you off occasionally rather than try to hide you. Hiding anyone merely invites speculation and suspicion. I learned that a long time ago.'

'What is this place?' she asked as he closed his big hand over hers and led her out onto a balcony set with a table for two and a waiter hovering in readiness.

'It's my penthouse apartment on the top floor. It's convenient and fully serviced without the need for further staff.'

'It's also very beautiful,' Sunny savoured, standing by the wrought-iron railing to admire the view and note the boats chugging down the river far below them, boats crammed with tourists admiring the historic city by night, their cameras flashing, their bright chatter floating softly upward.

Raj placed his hands either side of hers where they were braced on the rail and then slowly eased his hands over hers. 'I thought you would like it.'

Insanely conscious of the heat of his big body at her back, Sunny laughed and quivered with awareness and a weakening yearning to simply lean back into him. 'I do but I'm also wondering how many times you've been here and you've been so lost in work that you didn't even take the time to appreciate the beauty.'

Raj grinned, drinking in the faint coconut scent drifting up from her hair. 'That's why you're here,' he told her shamelessly. 'To keep me grounded… to show me everything I fail to notice around me.'

The warmth of him was spreading through her like a dangerous drug, lighting up pathways she had worked hard to shut down again weeks earlier. Raj, for that one sultry night, had been an indulgence, but the whole point of an indulgence was that it should be a very, very occasional treat because to repeat indulgences too often was to be self-destructive. And Sunny reminded herself that she was much too sensible for that sort of behaviour, particularly when she was pregnant.

Champagne was being uncorked by the waiter and Sunny thought fast and told a hurried lie. 'I'm on these tablets right now that mean I shouldn't touch alcohol. I don't want to be a party pooper but I would rather not drink.'

'Not a problem.' Raj waved away the champagne and suggested that they sit down and start their meal.

'Sorry about that,' Sunny muttered as she sipped her water, still feeling ashamed of the lie she had told to conceal her condition. He would understand later but this seemingly special dinner, staged high above the grandeur of the river Seine, was neither the right moment nor the right place in which to make such a very personal and private announcement.

'Don't apologise on my behalf, because I seldom drink. My father was a heavy drinker. I suspect he was an alcoholic and that that powered his violent temper and his mistreatment of my mother and me,' he intoned grimly. 'If *that* is in my genes, I should be careful.'

They ate delicious starters and embarked on the main course. Why, Sunny was wondering, did this appear to be a meal that was celebrating something? She was bemused. It felt as though she had missed some crucial line of dialogue at some stage, ensuring that everything after it seemed oddly out of sync. She drank the fruit juice that was brought to her and concentrated on her tender steak. When the dessert arrived, she toyed with hers.

Raj closed a hand over hers. 'Come closer.'

Sunny's eyes opened very wide. 'Er…why?' she mumbled.

Raj's gaze welded to the generous swell of her firm breasts and then up to her soft pink luscious mouth. 'I want to hold you,' he said frankly. 'Obviously.'

Obviously? Since when was that requirement obvious? He dismissed the waiter, said he'd call for coffee and reached for Sunny. He was so strong that he literally lifted her out of her chair to bring her down on his spread thighs with a growly sound of satisfaction that reverberated through his chest. 'That's better. Now watch the fireworks,' he told her.

What fireworks? she almost asked, but a split second later fireworks were shooting up into the night sky and bursting into brilliant multicoloured flowers in the most breathtaking display. 'Those are so pretty…they even have pastel ones. Pansy would adore this.'

'We'll do this with her another time.'

Sunny rested back in his arms, shocked that she had settled there without argument, but he felt so good and he made her feel so safe. 'You knew the fireworks would be on,' she guessed.

'I put them on for you,' Raj corrected.

Sunny twisted on his lap and awkwardly peered at his hard profile. 'But why would you do that?'

'Because I felt like it…and because you can be very slow on the uptake, Sunny,' he spelt out softly, his mouth dropping down to a sensitive spot on her nape and dallying there until tiny little quivers of response were running through her like a river in full flood. 'Something I'm only now finding out.'

'What are you saying?' Sunny almost whispered.

Expelling his breath in a measured hiss, Raj thrust his chair back and lifted her again, lowering her to the floor to stand before him. 'This whole evening… you *still* haven't got the message?' he breathed almost incredulously.

'What message?' she asked, held captive by dark eyes flaming gold like a tiger's.

'There are now *no* other women in my life,' Raj imparted with precision. 'That term was what we negotiated…and now we have a deal, signed, sealed and delivered.'

Sunny was shattered. She stood there, anxious lavender-blue eyes locked to him in dawning comprehension. 'I told you that relationships don't come under the deal heading.'

Raj groaned out loud. 'And I told you I'd never had a relationship before. But you and I…*that's* a deal. It took me longer than I expected to settle the mistresses and remove them from my life but I haven't been with any of them since I met you, so that's exclusive, right?' A questioning ebony brow lifted.

'Right,' she agreed limply, because she truly could not think of anything else to say when he had stunned her stupid and her legs felt like cotton-wool supports because she had never ever envisaged being in the situation he had now placed her in. 'I can't believe you went to all that trouble for me.'

'I want you. And when I want something as much as I want you I will do whatever it takes to make it happen.'

'Obviously,' she said shakily. 'But I really wasn't expecting this development. I agreed to be with you for *one* night, not anything like this!'

'Understandably, I made certain assumptions of my own,' Raj fielded.

'Oh, that doesn't surprise me in the slightest!' Sunny flung back at him, breathless with lingering shock and disbelief. She had tried to keep him at a distance. She had put up barriers but Raj had rolled over the top of her barriers like an enemy tank. Entirely off his own bat, he had shelved his mistresses in apparent favour of her alone.

But how could that possibly work in the future? Eventually, he would get tired of her, of course he would, and then everything with Pansy would become horribly awkward because, in the aftermath, neither of them was likely to want to see the other.

'And what about when we break up again? How is that likely to affect Pansy?' Sunny demanded.

Raj groaned. 'Why is Sunny the optimist considering worst-case scenarios here? We're adults, we'll remain civil and it won't have the smallest effect on our niece.'

Sunny breathed in deep and slow, calming, composing herself.

'This isn't a game, Sunny. I don't play games. What I like about you is that you're honest with me about what you want, what you expect, and I will *try* to deliver,' Raj told her with roughened sincerity. 'But I'll get it wrong sometimes. I hate failure but it's human to fail. I like perfect the best and, so far, this evening has been perfect.'

Only it wouldn't be perfect any more if she practised that honesty he liked so much about her. Everything would fall apart in the instant she admitted that she had conceived his child. He wouldn't see the miracle that she saw, no, he would see a betrayal of trust, because she had naïvely assured him that she couldn't get pregnant. Only she hadn't known that there even *could* be a risk of that development.

She was torn in two at the prospect of having to tell him. No, not at this moment when he was smiling, when he had got rid of the other women in his life to make a special place for her, when he had put on flowery fireworks purely for her benefit. How could she allow him to have surrendered so much for a reward like that? He wouldn't see their unborn child as a reward. Raj viewed life and people through a different lens.

'And now it's about to get even more perfect,' Raj concluded, vaulting upright with a slashing wicked smile that made her heart pound. He scooped her up into his arms with ease and strode back indoors, ignoring her gasp of surprise as he strode through double doors into a bedroom fit for a queen. Her troubled gaze flicked over gleaming contemporary furniture, lamplit pools of privacy and the biggest bed she had ever seen draped in white linen. Through the windows she could see the fireworks still throwing up colourful blossoms. She would tell him about the baby in the morning, she decided, when things were calm again and he was in a more receptive mood.

'I've been thinking of this moment multiple times a day for weeks,' Raj confided as he knelt down on one knee and flipped her shoes off with the utmost casualness.

'I never even got to thank you for the dress,' Sunny exclaimed, suddenly shy at the prospect of being stripped naked, wondering if he would notice the subtle differences that were already changing her body. Her breasts were larger, and, goodness knew, she hadn't needed nature's help there, and there was a very faint curve now to her tummy, which had previously been flat.

'I saw a picture of it and it was *you*,' Raj told her, dropping his jacket where he stood, yanking off his tie, all action and impatience now that what he saw as the formalities had all been taken care of.

Yet Sunny seemed to still be in shock because she was as yet showing him none of the relief and satisfaction he had somehow expected. He had embraced celibacy for many weeks for her, had focused on the goal and that goal was acquiring Sunny at any cost. And even before he dared to lay a finger on her, he knew that she was worth it, he knew that she wanted to be with him because he was the man that he was, because she *cared*, and he had never had that before. She didn't want him to take her out and show her off, she didn't want the public recognition that could drive normal people to insanity, she didn't want the money and all that it could buy, she only wanted *him*. And in Raj's world, that made her a pearl beyond price.

CHAPTER SEVEN

SUNNY WATCHED RAJ haul off his shirt, revealing his magnificent, bronzed torso, not to mention all the pure, defined lines of his pecs and abs. He was in superb physical condition and she knew that one of these days there would be a sketch pad in her hand and she would be drawing him in charcoal, shading in the angles and the hollows of his lean, athletic body. He was beautiful, from his sharp as diamond cheekbones to his deep-set dark golden eyes and the sensually alluring curve of his lips...and he wanted her, *her*, she reflected in sheer wonderment.

Nobody had ever wanted her enough to make sacrifices for her...except, perhaps, her mother, she conceded ruefully. Refusing to terminate her pregnancy, Sunny's mother had protected the child that her husband didn't want, the child that Sunny's father had feared might cost money that he saw as more properly belonging to her half-sister Christabel's needs. But that sacrifice had pretty much cost her mother her marriage, although her mother had been clear that that marriage had been on the rocks by then owing to her father's complete absorption in Christabel and his management of her career.

And then there had been Jack, who had turned his back on the love he'd said he had for her to find a fertile woman who could give him the children he craved. Fortunately for his wife, she had had no problems falling pregnant, but how would he have reacted if conception had not been that easy? Raj, on the other hand, hadn't seen her as being less of a woman because she had believed that she was infertile, but then he had never hoped to have children with her anyway. Only, how would he feel now when she finally confessed the truth? In despair, she banished that hovering black cloud of fear and dissension from her mind to concentrate on the present.

Shedding his trousers, Raj came down on the bed beside her and flipped her over to run down the zip on her dress before proceeding to extract her from it with single-minded intent. As she tumbled back against the pillows, he smoothed her rumpled hair and studied her with satisfaction. The smooth slopes of her firm breasts were cradled in blue silk and lace.

'It's almost a crime to take this off you,' he husked, reaching under her for the clasp to detach the bra. 'You have to know that you look amazing…all that smooth glowing skin.'

'I must've got the sun in Italy.'

'How? You were clothed from head to foot,' he scoffed.

And she smiled secretively, wondering if there was

truth in that old chestnut about a pregnancy glow. The bra was trailed off and she succumbed to her shyness, wrenching back the smooth sheet to scramble below its cover.

'You're no fun,' Raj complained, amused by her bashfulness, cupping her cheek in one large hand to ravish her mouth hungrily with his while he tossed the sheet back, and then long fingers strolled across her hip down to the silk-clad triangle covering her mons.

Sunny quivered as he skated a fingertip over the most sensitive spot of all and pervasive heat began to rise between her legs. He traced an achingly tender nipple with the edge of his teeth and she shuddered, suddenly on fire for him, arms reaching up to pull him closer.

'I like it when you lose control of that prim nature,' he growled.

'I'm not prim.'

'It's not a bad thing, not a criticism. I'm more accustomed to the opposite trait and I'm not a fan of that either. I only need you to be yourself with me.'

'I don't know how to be anything else.'

While she was gazing up into his stunning eyes, he tugged up her knees and disposed of her last garment before shimmying down the bed with lithe grace and sliding between her thighs.

He traced her seam with the tip of his tongue and then moved on with fervour to explore all that lay between. She gasped and arched and he held her down, his hands firm on her hips while he subjected her to the most merciless onslaught of pleasure she had ever experienced. And then the pace slowed as he circled her clitoris and even before he slid a finger into the molten depths of her she was moaning and crying out as a climax took her by storm, shaking her body with waves of drowning bliss.

'You're really quick at that,' Raj remarked with unwelcome amusement.

'You're too good at it.'

'I've only done that with you...at least since I was seduced and taught the basics by an older woman when I was fourteen.'

She frowned. 'That was too young.'

'I was too young for most of the things I was surrounded by at university. It was inevitable that some young woman would wonder what the kid nerd would be like in bed, and I was curious enough to accept the invitation,' he admitted.

'Wrong, all the same.'

'I was a lonely kid. Any kind of interaction with another student meant something to me.'

'I hate the idea of that.' Sunny explored his parted lips with her own, slowly, delicately, until Raj took over, delving deep, twining his tongue with hers over and over until hunger began to engulf her again.

Strong and sure, he came down on her, lifting her legs, pushing against her where she was most tender. He entered her with a raw groan of pleasure, stretching her tight walls, seating himself deep, and then he began to move. Her heart hammering, she arched up to him, struggling to contain the raw excitement sending flames of feverish impatience hurtling through her. He settled into a rhythm, shifted, changed his angle, drove her a little insane while the pressure mounted and tightened inside her. And then, in the midst of that heated desperate climb to satisfaction, he turned her over, pulled her up on her knees and pounded back into her with relentless energy. Just as suddenly she reached that peak and he pushed her over it. She stifled a scream in the padded headboard, her heart racing so fast that she was convinced she would stop breathing there and then. With a deep groan of fulfilment, he pulled back from her.

'OK?' Raj tugged her back down into the bed, spread her limp body out and tugged the sheet over her. 'I'll want you again soon but you're tired. Nap for a while.'

Tired? She felt as though her entire body had been wired and then somebody had yanked out all the wires that made her limbs work. She was a boneless, weightless doll but her conscience was heavier than lead at the same time. She would tell him about the baby in the morning.

'What are you thinking about?' she asked him abstractedly.

His brow furrowed. 'The fireworks were naff. I would have preferred to use synchronised drones but I would've needed a lot of them and getting permission in an urban area like this would have been a major headache...'

Ask a man, get an answer, she thought ruefully. 'I loved the fireworks.'

'I'll run a bath for you,' Raj announced with sudden energy, vaulting out of the bed and striding through one of the doors.

Gushing water sounded and then she heard him using his phone, talking fast in fluent French. A little while later someone rang a bell. Raj strode through the bedroom, a towel wrapped round his lean waist, and strode back again, a giant box in his arms. 'The bath's almost ready,' he told her, waking her up on the very edge of sleep.

A little while later, Raj scooped her out of the bed and carried her into the bathroom. Giant gilded impressive candelabra filled with candles flamed all around a sunken bath with a steaming surface covered with rose petals and flowers. It was as magnificent as a film stage set and it took her breath away. He set her down and guided her down the steps into the bath.

'Do you really like this sort of nonsense?' he enquired critically half under his breath.

'Oh...yes,' she admitted, sinking happily into the warm water.

'Sorry it took so long. They had to get me candles and holders and all that jazz,' he complained.

'It was truly worth it. Thank you,' she whispered

weakly, shaken by the effort he had made on her behalf.

Raj smiled and her heart squeezed inside her tight chest. She was falling in love with him and she knew she couldn't control her emotions around him. He was everything she had ever dreamt of but nothing that she had ever expected to find. In action he had a sort of hurricane effect, all bristling energy and determination, but underneath the seething impatience and exasperation with the world's difficulties was an absolutely wonderful guy.

'You're amazing,' she said softly as he walked back out of the bathroom.

Raj stopped dead and wheeled round to look back at her with hard dark eyes. 'I don't do soppy, Sunny. I don't have those feelings to give. I've never felt them for anyone.'

Well, that was telling her, but taking that onboard after the evening they had shared was still a challenge. The glorious fireworks, the intimacy, the fabulous bath? Nothing special in his estimation, it seemed. And didn't that fact just give her an even more huge gulf to cross with him in the morning when she finally told him that she had conceived?

Sunny blew out the candles one by one, made use of the towelling robe on offer and moved back into the bedroom. Raj was seated by the television watching the business news in front of a trolley of food.

'You're eating again?' she teased, having decided to ignore that crack that he didn't do soppy. Not a denial worth taking seriously, she thought, not when she'd had the flowery fireworks and the equally flowery candlelit bath.

'Being with you makes me hungry.' He sprang upright and simply reached for her in the same motion, lifting her up into his arms and settling down again with her as if such behaviour were perfectly normal.

'Is that an achievement?' she whispered helplessly.

'It hasn't happened before.' Yanking over the trolley with one relaxed foot, Raj reached for a plate and passed it to her, offering her selections, pushing his own favourite snacks. 'You're a healthy eater.'

'And you're surprised?'

'Nothing about you surprises me.'

Oh, just you wait until tomorrow, she reflected unhappily, thinking of the baby on board without his awareness and that seemed wrong to her, that she still hadn't told him, that she was holding off on that ground-breaking news for the right moment. And in truth there *was* no right moment for that kind of news. Her surprise was likely to stretch far beyond anything he had envisaged and breach his trust and relaxation in her company. Once he knew, everything would change in his attitude and *that* was why she was staying silent, she acknowledged ruefully. She would happily live in their little cocoon of togetherness for a few hours more before she let reality in to burst the bubble.

He laid a gift-wrapped parcel onto her lap when

she had finished snacking. 'I picked it up in Geneva. It struck me as the sort of thing that you'd like.'

'You shouldn't keep buying me stuff...' she muttered uncomfortably, removing the wrapping paper with care to expose a leather folder. Opening it up, she discovered that it was a travelling sketchbook, one side holding the paper, the other the pencils. 'But this is perfect and so compact too. I'll be able to take it out and about with me. Thanks, but no more gifts, please.'

She fell asleep, only rousing when he slotted her into the cool bed, unwrapping her from the robe, ignoring her drowsy protests.

'You're a very restful woman to be with,' he told her.

'Because I keep on falling asleep?'

'No, because you don't feel the need to fill every silence with idle chatter.'

With a sleepy chuckle she burrowed into her pillows, luxuriating in the heat of him at her back. He wasn't holding her, certainly wasn't spooning her, but he was close and that was enough.

A light trail of kisses down her sensitive spine brought her to wakefulness. 'Hmm...' she framed. 'What time is it?'

'Dawn, best time of the day.'

'I'll take your word for it,' she mumbled, smothering a yawn.

His mouth explored the smooth slope of her shoulder and she squirmed back into the hard heat of his aroused physique. 'Oh…I should shower first.'

'No. You smell of me. I love that,' he growled, closing her into his arms, his big hands glancing across her sensitive nipples and unerringly tracing a fiery path to the damp heat at her core. 'I want you.'

Sunny parted her thighs in silent consent for him to continue and a roughened laugh coursed through his chest. He lifted her leg and sank into her with delicious strength and a soundless sigh escaped her parted lips. He went slow and deep and the excitement climbed through her pliant body in surge after surge until her heart was hammering and little moans were wrenched from her throat. It happened for both of them simultaneously. He slammed into her receptive channel one last time and her body shattered like glass into a writhing orgasm as he reached completion with her.

'Shower or bath?'

'Shower…but you keep your mittens off me,' she warned, suddenly recalling what still lay ahead of her and yet unable to regret a moment of the time they had spent together, lost in intimacy. At least she would have some memories to revisit after she had depth-charged their togetherness out of existence with the announcement she was about to make.

'No choice but to do so if we want to make it back early for Pansy,' he reminded her.

Reality felt as though it had a tight grip round her throat. She slid straight out of bed, grabbed up the robe, pushed her arms into the sleeves and reached the bathroom in record time. Within minutes she was showering, shampooing her hair, working out exactly what she would say to him over breakfast. She tugged on her jeans, wincing at the struggle she had to get the zip up. She completed the outfit with a multicoloured filmy loose blouse and stuck her feet into ballet flats.

Rain was pattering softly down on the balcony when she emerged and saw a table laid for breakfast in the main reception area. She breathed in deep and slow. As soon as they were alone, she murmured quietly, 'I have something important to tell you but I want to ask you to let me do the talking. Please don't rush into judgement. This isn't a scam or a con or anything that really requires your concern. Please don't interrupt me and please contain your reactions and allow yourself time to think in private about what I tell you. First and foremost, we have Pansy to consider and we need a good working relationship to achieve that. Angry words or accusations won't be soon forgotten, so that's why I'm asking you to take a deep breath and say nothing for now.'

His ebony brows had pleated. His lean strong face was taut. Her senses buzzed because he looked so achingly handsome. Her colour rose.

'Obviously, I'm intrigued,' he said.

'You won't be by the time I'm finished,' Sunny forecast heavily. 'When I was twelve years old I suffered a burst appendix and I almost died. Five years later, when I was seventeen, my mother informed me that I would never have children because of the damage done to my reproductive organs. At least, that is presumably what the doctor told her back then. I was shocked. So much that I had taken for granted was taken from me that night, and the next day, when I shared that news with my boyfriend, Jack, he dumped me. He had said he loved me but he wanted children and if I couldn't give him what he wanted, he didn't want me either.'

'Short-sighted.' Raj hadn't been joking when he'd said that he was intrigued. His first thought, which had sent his blood pressure rocketing, was that another man had come into her life. But he found that hard to believe. There was no reluctance in Sunny when she was with him, no sense that her loyalties were divided except when it came to their niece. And that he found perfectly acceptable. A con? A scam? What nonsense was she referring to? And why on earth was she choosing to begin with a detailed rendering of her infertility when he was already aware of her condition?

'Six weeks ago, we were together on your yacht and we were intimate without precautions. You thought it was safe. I also thought it was safe but when I went to the doctor a couple of weeks ago and had tests because I was feeling under par, I learned that I was pregnant.' Sunny rose from her chair and walked across the room. 'I was transfixed. I couldn't believe it. I argued, pointed out that it was impossible. He looked at my notes and told me that after the damage caused by my burst appendix, I had been lucky enough to have repairs carried out by a skilled surgeon…and clearly, I had healed. According to him, I should never have been told that I was infertile and that, at worst, I should only have been warned that I *might* have difficulty conceiving.'

'Sunny,' Raj began tautly, stormy dark eyes locked to her like an impending tidal wave.

'No…no, say nothing,' Sunny reminded him, actually shaking an admonitory finger at him, her voice a little shaky. 'For now, the floor is mine. Last night, you tore the ground out from under my feet. I wasn't expecting all *this*!' She stretched her arms wide to encompass their surroundings, the fireworks and the candlelit bath she would never forget. 'I was going to tell you last night. I wasn't expecting you to tell me that you had parted with the other women in your life. I assumed that, as far as you were concerned, I would be returning to simply being Pansy's aunt again. So, forgive me for not coming clean with you last night. I couldn't face it.

'Now…' Sunny spun back to him, golden hair flying round her flushed features '…let me get the factual stuff out of the way. I'm planning to have this baby and I'm very happy about it, just a little sorry that it's happened the way it has because that's unfortunate for you. You didn't get a choice but then I didn't either. We were both genuinely misled. I'm not considering a termination or adoption or any other option. I'm a strong, independent woman with decent earning power. I don't need anything from you. I don't *want* anything from you.'

'Sunny,' Raj gritted in interruption as he lost patience.

Violet eyes struck his in a heady collision. 'Keep quiet,' she warned him. 'I'm telling you everything you need to know and you should listen. This child need not change your life in any way. You won't need to acknowledge him or her or even see the child. This is *my* child, nothing whatsoever to do with you. I will never tell anyone who fathered my child. If pressured, I will say I had a regrettable one-night stand with a stranger.'

'Regrettable?' Raj growled with incredulous bite.

'Oh, don't take it personally. That's what I would say for the sake of a story that nobody would wish to question further. I don't regret that night, I *couldn't...*' Sunny's tense face suddenly lit up with a guilty smile and there was apology in her eyes as she looked at him. 'It was a wonderful night and it also gave me my heart's secret desire, so I'm never likely to complain about that.'

Raj gritted his teeth again. He saw the prospect of another deal looming in front of him. He would have to negotiate and compromise, and compromising had never come naturally to him. He liked to win. He hated losing. But then this was Sunny, hogtying him into a remarkably sensible silence to ensure that *he* said nothing rude or unforgivable. A...

baby. Her heart's desire, his biggest *fear*. The challenge of being a parent when he had never had a parent to respect. Not his hateful father, not the weak mother he had despised but supported out of loyalty and pity. A baby with Sunny, on the way and welcomed by her, at least.

He vaulted upright, relieved from the restraint of remaining silent. 'I don't see why this development should change anything between us,' he spelt out tautly.

Sunny moved forward, looking at him in apparent astonishment. 'But—'

'No, you've had the floor. Now it's my turn,' Raj pronounced gruffly as he locked his hands to her arms and pulled her unexpectedly close. 'There's nothing more to say on that topic for now. But I do need to ask you about hosting an event with me in ten days' time at my London base.'

'An…event?' Sunny whispered, struggling not to sound as though she was struggling with disbelief that he could simply move on and immediately leave her earth-shattering pregnancy announcement behind him.

'It's a fund-raising event for my charitable foundation. However, most of the events I throw are business related. I would appreciate your presence by my side for this one. We're a partnership now and it should be public,' he continued smoothly. 'I'll also organise a maternity wardrobe for you. It's a business expense, don't worry about it.'

Her lower lip parted from her upper in sheer awe

at his detachment. He hadn't reacted at all. He had stayed silent just as she had asked and how could she complain about that? Evidently her reassurances that she required no further input from him on the issue of her pregnancy had worked a treat. So, why was she now being ridiculously perverse and wanting to know what his *true* feelings were? After all, hadn't she barred him from expressing those feelings?

'You haven't eaten much for breakfast.'

'I wasn't very hungry,' she confided. 'Nerves got the better of me.'

'Am I that intimidating?' Raj asked softly.

Sunny reddened uncomfortably. 'No, of course not, but I had worked myself up into a real tizz over things.'

'No need. I'm steady as a rock in a crisis. Lived through too many of them to be anything else,' he fielded lightly, easing her even closer while she was wondering if that word 'crisis' was a hint as to his hidden reactions to the news that he was going to become a father.

Raj shifted his hips against her and she stilled, feeling in shock the hard thrust of his arousal even through their clothes. Maybe a crisis turned him on, she thought limply.

'So, if you're not planning to eat anything more, I wondered if…?'

'You're a very demanding guy,' she muttered unevenly.

'And you can be a very demanding woman,' he

told her before he dropped his head and kissed her breathless with a ravishing hunger that blew her away.

'Have we…er…got time?' she almost whispered, shame and self-consciousness holding her still and uncertain.

He hoisted her up against him and carried her back into the bedroom and began calmly divesting her of her clothes. 'Jeans are too hard to get you out of,' he complained.

'Won't wear them again,' she mumbled, still stunned by the developments taking place. 'I prefer skirts and these are too tight now.'

'Shush,' Raj hushed her with the heat and passion of his mouth on hers again and excitement raced through her like a rejuvenating drug. She sat up on the bed and began to wrench at his Brioni suit with unappreciative hands. 'You want me?'

'So much,' she said with a helpless shiver.

'I want you the same way,' Raj drawled without hesitation. 'I won't let this development come between us.'

And, half dressed, he pinned her to the bed and took her with raw passion and her climax was breathtaking. All the relief she was experiencing, all the fear she had buried drove her higher and higher and she was splintering into a million pieces when Raj finally pulled away and muttered that it was time to get to the airfield.

'Er…this maternity wardrobe,' she framed uneasily. 'I don't intend to be your newest mistress.'

'If you stand by my side, you should be wearing clothes that ensure that nobody can try to diminish your status in my life,' Raj declared squarely. 'And although it's superficial, people do judge by appearances and I will not allow you to put yourself in a lowly position.'

'So, the clothes will be more for your benefit than mine.'

'You've got it. And by the way,' Raj continued levelly, 'I don't often appear with a woman in public, unless she's an employee, and you will also be acting as my hostess, so why would anyone assume that you are merely a mistress?'

Sunny groaned. 'This sounds like an awful lot to take on…will it be worth the hassle?'

Raj froze and spun back to her as she tried to zip up her jeans again and conceal the fact that it was a struggle for her to do so. 'Am I worth it?' he shot back at her. 'You are worth it to me.'

And Sunny nodded in agreement, dazed by him, her body still singing with pleasure and a steadily mounting sense of peace. He hadn't made a four-act tragedy out of her unexpected pregnancy. He hadn't doubted that the baby was his…at least, she didn't think so. He was taking her fertility in his stride because that was Raj, who would storm on past while other people were still trying to work out what was coming next. She decided that that was a surprisingly soothing response.

They were back at Ashton Hall by mid-morning and Pansy ran across the hall to welcome her back. Scooped up into Sunny's arms, she accepted a hug and reached out a hand to Raj in greeting, grabbing at his sleeve. In response he lifted the little girl from Sunny and swung her high. The hall rang with her delighted chuckles. He suggested taking his niece down to the home farm on the Ashton estate and Sunny was impressed. He had listened when she'd told him how much Pansy enjoyed seeing animals and had already organised a suitable outing.

When they got back to the house, a fashion buyer, organised by Raj, was waiting to see her to take her measurements and consult her preferences in colour and style. The speed with which everything happened on Raj's orders left her breathless. She acquiesced, told herself that she had to adapt to a certain extent, had to at least try and fit in. Just look at how fast he had appeared to adapt to the prospect of a baby! If he could make the effort, so could she, she reasoned.

But *had* Raj adapted? Or was he simply ignoring what he had referred to as 'a development'? There was nothing personal about that attitude. It seemed as though he would accept the baby because he wanted *her* and she had made it clear that she expected nothing more from him. Who could tell what the future would bring? He was granting her the independence she had requested and how could she complain about that? Everything that happened would be her choice and surely that was reassuring?

That evening they dined in the grand dining room, just the two of them. As they went upstairs, Raj caught her hand in his as she would have veered left to her bedroom. 'I had the staff move your stuff while we ate,' he imparted. 'You sleep with me now.'

Sunny swallowed hard. 'And that's it? We don't even discuss it?' she exclaimed.

'What is there to discuss? We're together and we have no reason to hide the fact,' he pointed out, sounding perfectly logical.

Sunny breathed in slow and deep. 'I'm starting to feel a little taken over, like my life's not mine any more,' she admitted unevenly.

Raj shot her a hard appraisal. 'You're as free as you've always been. All the choices are yours to make.'

'It's just all happening so fast. I suppose I don't like change,' she muttered uncertainly as he released her hand in the manner of a male who had forgotten he was holding it and now regretted ever touching it in the first place.

She could see him mentally stepping back from her and she hated it. She decided it wasn't the moment to take a stance, particularly not when all her belongings had been removed from the room she had been using. 'Never mind. I'm just having a bit of a wobble. I'll get over it,' she insisted, moving on by his side.

'No,' Raj said quietly. 'I think you still have to decide whether or not you want to be with me and embrace all the baggage that comes with me.'

'Right.' Sunny hovered and then followed him. 'I don't like it when you read me that accurately.'

Raj thrust open the door on a massive well-appointed bedroom. 'I've got some work to catch up on,' he said casually. 'I'll see you later.'

And he just left her there, marooned in the centre of the huge room. She wandered into the bathroom and found nothing that belonged to her, eventually discovering a second bathroom that contained her toiletries. The few clothes she had brought were stowed in a separate dressing room. Everything was separate, she realised. He liked his own space too. After a few minutes of uncertainty, she got undressed and finally climbed into the comfortable bed.

Raj was annoyed with her. She knew that. He made decisions lightning fast and expected her to react just as quickly. But that wasn't her nature. He had decided that he wanted her and had met her unwitting demands by getting rid of the other women in his life. But she hadn't known that he would be *willing* to do that, hadn't ever stopped to think what it would mean to *be* with him in a relationship because that had not seemed to be a possibility a few weeks earlier.

So, obviously, having gone to such lengths, Raj

expected her to fully accept what she had got herself into and not dilly-dally on the edges of his life fussing about every new step he put in front of her. She was supposed to fall into place automatically. And did she want to do that? Did she want Raj enough to stride boldly into the unknown? Was she just a coward? Or was she trying to protect herself? After all, nobody got to control the future.

And she was already halfway to being in love with him, even if he didn't do 'soppy'. Bailing out at this stage would be foolish, especially when she would be forced to keep on seeing him, particularly when she carried his baby.

She lay alone in the bed for a long time and when he finally came to bed he was quiet and he didn't come close to her at all. She had screwed up. Maybe he had expected her to be pleased and flattered when he moved her into his bedroom. After all, it was quite a statement and it was very Raj, who would refuse to sneak around in his own house when he had nothing to hide. But that statement he had made had, ironically, divided them.

'I've decided that I'm all in,' Sunny admitted as he watched her and Pansy getting in the car to leave the next morning.

His rare smile lit up his lean, darkly handsome face. 'You won't regret it,' he swore.

CHAPTER EIGHT

'I'LL SEE YOU tonight when you arrive and I'll probably rip your clothes off in the first hour,' Raj warned her on the back of a groan. 'It's been a *very* long few days.'

Flushed and with helpless heat coiling in her pelvis like a welcome party, Sunny came off the phone again and walked back into the kitchen where Gemma was pouring tea.

'Was that Raj?' her neighbour asked.

'And you'll be seeing him tonight,' Gemma remarked. 'But it'll still be a challenge conducting a long-distance relationship. He seems to travel all over the place.'

'Yes, I'll learn as I go,' Sunny said lightly. 'And thanks again for stepping into the breach with the animals this evening. I don't mind asking you occasionally, but I don't plan to do it as regularly as this. I'll make other arrangements.'

Gemma assured her that it wasn't a problem but Sunny knew the difference between an occasional favour and a regular demand on someone's time and was determined not to continue putting the other woman out. She had acquired her animals. Her two dogs—Bert was beginning to look more and more like a permanent member of the household—and her cat and her horse, not to mention the ducks saved from certain death when they were dropped off in a box at her gate. She had taken them all in when she was a regular stay-at-home, who rarely went anywhere. They remained her responsibility, nobody else's.

She wondered what her friend would say once she realised that Sunny was pregnant. There would be a lot of gossip and curious looks and she would simply have to deal with it. There was no need to justify a baby she was over the moon to be carrying or defend herself when it was no longer unusual for a woman to choose to have a baby alone. It was, as Raj would say, merely 'a development'.

She drove herself down to London, singing nursery rhymes to Pansy and pointing out animals when the little girl got bored. Raj's London base was a massive house on the Thames. Even getting into the grounds past the security meant being checked off a list and having her car boot searched. Pansy began to grizzle, tired and hungry and fed up.

'Miss Barker…' An older woman dressed in black awaited her at the front door. 'I'm Beth, Mr Belanger's housekeeper.'

She was ushered in like visiting royalty to find that Maria was already waiting for their arrival. The nanny pounced on Pansy and grinned when Sunny told her that her niece needed food and possibly a nap. As Pansy was carried off, Sunny was shown upstairs to the master bedroom suite where she knew all her new clothes would be stored. She flicked through them, finally extracting a long gown in the finest dark blue lace. It was neatly tailored to allow a little more space over the tummy while shaping her other curves. Having previewed the dress online, she had already decided that she would wear it for Raj's event and, rummaging through her new shoe collection, she extracted a navy pair of heels in triumph.

Raj stalked in. 'You're here!' he proclaimed with satisfaction.

'I was working out what to wear tonight,' she told him while wondering how he could look so good with his black hair tousled and his jawline darkly shadowed by stubble. He looked what he was: a very powerful masculine tycoon, awash with volatile energy and buckets of raw sex appeal. Studying him, a visceral tug clenching at the heart of her, she stilled a shiver that had nothing to do with being cold.

'It's been a long week.' He raked long brown fingers through his unruly black hair. 'I didn't expect to miss you.'

Raj almost made that sound like an accusation, as if she should've been with him rather than away from him.

'I'm here now,' she parried lightly. 'Have you seen Pansy yet?'

'She waved her toast at me. She was too busy eating to give me much attention. I'll spend time with her tomorrow.'

'I'm afraid we have to leave early tomorrow morning. I have a painting commission and the buyer's in a hurry.'

Raj lifted an imperious brow. 'The buyer will have to wait.'

'No, I agreed to work with his time limit,' Sunny broke in.' It's his mother's favourite flower and it's for her birthday. I need to make a start on it tomorrow. I'm delighted that it will be finding a home with someone who will truly appreciate it.'

His shapely sexy mouth tightened. 'I'm already a keen convert. I've got a glorified weed hanging above my bed. I truly appreciate it too for all that intricate detail.'

And she finally noticed that it was her painting hanging there on the wall and she smiled with pleasure that he had given it a place in his bedroom. She moved closer, almost mesmerised by the pulsing masculine energy and charisma of him that close and the way that aura pulled her in. 'I missed you too but I can't keep on taking so much time away from home. I have to work. I have to look after my animals.'

'We'll discuss all that later,' Raj asserted. 'Right now I only want—'

'To rip my clothes off? Please don't rip anything,' she said very seriously. 'Until I take possession of my new wardrobe…thank you, by the way…I'm low on clothes that fit and most of the stuff in the new wardrobe is fancy stuff for when I'm with you.'

His big hands framed her cheekbones. 'Stop fussing. I promise there will be no ripping of any kind,' he swore very seriously as he whipped her top over her head and dropped it on the floor and went looking for the zip on her jeans.

'Why are your jeans so big?'

'To allow for expansion,' she muttered in embarrassment, rolling the elasticated waist of her maternity jeans down over her hips, mortified by his question. She might not have expanded quite enough to need actual maternity wear but her own clothing was already too tight for comfort.

He tipped up her chin and his mouth came crashing down with passionate force on hers, his tongue darting deep into the sensitive interior of her mouth, and a long shudder racked her, heat and craving infiltrating her with fresh energy.

Raj lifted her off her feet and laid her on the bed, flipping off her shoes and yanking off her jeans with scant ceremony. He surveyed her with maddening intensity. 'You are fit for this, aren't you? Maybe you're too tired or not well?' he suggested awkwardly, and it was an endearing awkwardness, as if he was unaccustomed to making such personal enquiries.

Sunny stretched up and yanked him by his tie down to her level. 'I'm ready and willing and you promised me.'

A smile slashed Raj's stubborn, wilful mouth. 'I did, didn't I?'

His hands found hers and pinned them to the bed while he kissed her with fiery hunger. The whole time she was conscious of the mobile phone buzzing in his pocket. Finally, he wrenched his lips from hers, sucked in oxygen and answered the call, speaking in brief sentences as he levered himself back off the bed. He dug the phone back in his pocket.

'I've overbooked you,' he groaned. 'We have no time for this no matter how much I want you.'

'You've overbooked *me*?' As Sunny sat up tense with incomprehension, Raj lifted her discarded garments, shook them out and set them carefully beside her. 'Get dressed,' he urged.

'Are you joking?'

'Only wish I were but you need time to dress for our guests and I also need you to come downstairs right now to look at something,' he told her ruefully.

Sunny stole a doubtful glance at the arousal tenting the fine fabric of his tailored trousers and reddened. 'You'd better close your jacket.'

'I'm sorry. I got carried away.' He sighed, shooting her a burnished dark look of hungry regret.

Sunny got dressed again in a hurry and then gasped in horror when she saw her reflection. Having tidied her mussed hair, she followed him back downstairs into an imposing drawing room. Raj settled her down in a seat. Two men lugging a chained metal security box entered and settled it at his feet before beginning to unlock it.

'It's a rare blue diamond. I wanted to see if it suited you.'

A pendant was lifted out of another internal box with reverent care and Raj swept it up to thread it round her neck. Sunny squinted down at the glittering stone.

'Look at me,' he urged.

And she did.

'I'll take it,' Raj pronounced with satisfaction.

'I can't accept this…' she hissed at him, stretching up to his ear as she began to unclasp the item.

'It's an investment,' Raj declared.

Sunny cradled the magnificent diamond nervously in the palm of her hand. 'It's the most amazing blue.'

'The boron atoms in the carbon atoms,' he explained. 'It reflects your eyes.'

'I can't accept something this valuable as a gift.'

'I want you to wear it this evening.'

'OK, but I'm not keeping it. Be warned…it'll only be round my neck on loan and as a favour to you.'

Troubled by the appearance of so evidently expensive a jewel, Sunny checked on Pansy, who was in her bath with Maria looking after her, before heading for the shower and working on her own presentation. Fully dressed and feeling very fancy, she picked her passage down the stairs in her high heels, the glorious diamond glittering below her collarbone like a breathtaking statement of wealth and exclusivity.

Raj strolled towards her, brilliant dark eyes radiating satisfaction. 'You look magnificent.'

'Thank you, but I'm starting to feel just a little too like a dress-up doll,' she confided in a low voice. 'Like I'm not really allowed to be me any more.'

Raj frowned and a photographer stepped forward to take photos of them as well as record the arrival of the most important guests. The evening was aimed at raising funds for Raj's charitable foundation and, in particular, a chain of children's hospices. Sunny recognised occasional well-known faces from the media and strove not to get self-conscious when Raj introduced her to everyone as his hostess. She saw the curiosity roused by that label and the attention commanded by the guiding hand he kept clamped to her spine. Drinks were served in the ballroom, all the catering handled by uniformed professionals. Speeches were made before the buffet was opened and it turned into a glitzy social occasion.

Raj was constantly mobbed. Beautiful women in over-the-top revealing dresses endeavoured to catch his eye and sparkle with jokes and one-liners, touching his arms, any part of him they could decently reach, striving to make a connection with him. Meanwhile, Sunny felt as though she was on display like a show pony. Her diamond pendant was repeatedly oohed and aahed over and she learned that it was a famous diamond, mined in Australia. The superb pendant began to feel like an albatross weighing down her neck. Whenever sheer curiosity prompted someone to try and get into closer conversation with her, Raj whisked her away, shielding her from everybody.

'It's nobody's business who you are,' he pointed out. 'That's private.'

'I've got nothing to be ashamed of, nothing to hide,' Sunny told him gently. 'And it's not a private event, because official photos are being taken at every turn.'

'It's my role to protect you,' Raj informed her with finality.

Sunny pictured a coffin lid slamming down on top of her. Raj would be happiest to lock her in a box and it would be *his* box, kept locked and accessible only to him. He needed to learn that she had spent a lot of time tied to home by her grandmother's declining health and, although she would willingly make that same sacrifice again, she would not make that same sacrifice of freedom or independence for any man alive. She valued her ability to do as she liked, wear what she liked, speak to whom she liked and no way would Raj be allowed to deprive her of those choices. She had been willing to make adjustments to fit in with his lifestyle but she wasn't prepared to give way to every demand and expectation.

'I've been thinking about your idea of leaving early tomorrow,' Raj mused later that evening when the last guests had departed.

'It wasn't an idea,' Sunny pointed out on the way upstairs, where she paused on the landing to step out of her shoes and carry them, flexing her pinched toes. 'It was a decision and it's already done and dusted.'

'There are *other* options,' Raj imparted as he thrust open the door of their bedroom. 'Don't close your mind to the alternatives or the solution.'

'No, there aren't any other options, not when it comes to my commissions and taking care of Pansy and my animals,' Sunny replied briskly, refusing to be drawn into a dialogue when she had no intention of changing her stance. 'I can only do those things at home.'

'I have a file for you to look over…a property file,' Raj told her, level dark eyes resting on her bemused gaze with a curious air of expectancy.

'I'm not moving anywhere. I'm staying put where I am.' Disconcerted by that new mystifying turn to the conversation, Sunny became even more tense.

'I think I could change your mind about that.' Raj swept a fat file off a nearby table and extended it to her. 'Skim over it and see. I own a lot of property and I can staff any one of them for you.'

'Well, you *would* think that you could change my mind, but you'd be wrong in this instance. My goodness, Raj, you could talk your way out of your allotted place in heaven and end up in the depths of hell out of pure obstinacy. You don't take a hint, you're relentless…quit while you're ahead!' she advised, moving her hand out of range of the file and walking into the bathroom she had been using.

She was letting herself get worked up and she told

herself off for not hanging onto her cool, but Raj had the capacity to make her feel cornered and she had no intention of letting him get away with that. Grabbing up her toiletries bag, she gathered up her necessities and then paused to detach the diamond at her throat. She set it down on the dresser top and padded on into the dressing room, where she retrieved her own clothes and nightwear and fresh underwear for the next morning.

'What on earth are you doing?' Raj demanded fiercely. 'What are we arguing about?'

'You're clever enough to know the answer to that question,' Sunny replied, wrapping her possessions together into a bundle, toiletries bag clutched awkwardly below one arm as she tried to sidestep him. 'I'm not sleeping in here with you.'

'Sunny!' As she opened the door to leave, he stalked after her. 'If you walk out of here right now, I will be angry with you.'

'And if I don't walk out, I'll be guilty of murder,' she confided tightly, hurrying down the corridor to the room she had used before.

Since she had taken off her shoes, her dress was trailing and she tripped up on the hem. She went sprawling with a gasp of fright, her belongings flying everywhere. Tears of frustration burned the backs of her eyes as she began to pick herself up again, grateful she hadn't hurt herself. A hand at her elbow, Raj levered her upright with care and crouched down to snatch up some of the stuff she had dropped as she did the same.

'This is crazy. I don't do scenes like this,' he censured.

'That's why I left your room,' Sunny said with as much dignity as she could muster, bundling everything up again.

'You could've fallen down the stairs.'

'But I *didn't*.' Sunny thrust open the door of the room she was determined to use.

Raj watched her lift her nose in the air, her chin at an angle, her spine rigid. What the hell was he supposed to have done? Frustration and impatience combined inside him, making him feel explosive.

He settled the property file down at the foot of the bed where she could browse through it once she had calmed down. Sunny dropped her clothing on the bed and carted the toiletries bag into the en suite bathroom.

'Tell me what I did,' he gritted, lounging back against the door to close it with a push of his big shoulders. 'Shouldn't I at least know what I'm supposed to have done?'

'You warned me that you hadn't been in a relationship before. I should have listened more, expected less. I feel like you're trying to take me over by stealth,' Sunny admitted unhappily. 'I'm not a business acquisition, Raj. I'm not a problem you have to cure, a breakage you have to fix. I'll never be perfect and that's fine with me but maybe it's not fine with you. Maybe you're only able to be satisfied with a sophisticate in a fancy designer dress with a whopping great diamond round her throat.'

'It was a business event and you wore a normal evening outfit. I wanted you to feel that you fitted in to improve your confidence.'

'There's nothing wrong with my confidence,' Sunny lied, unwilling to cede that she had felt more at ease during the evening because she had blended in with the other guests. 'But I have a life and I like my life as it is. I knew I would have to make allowances to fit into your life and I've done that. I'm travelling. I'm leaving my animals. I'm cutting my working hours back. I'm wearing the clothes you insisted on buying me. I even wore that diamond tonight to please you. But I'm *not* moving house for your benefit. I'm *not* prepared to keep on handing Pansy to a nanny for your benefit either!'

'Be fair, Sunny,' Raj urged. 'Maria has generally only looked after Pansy at bedtime and when you're in bed yourself. You're entitled to use an occasional babysitter when you're with her the rest of the time.'

'But when will you make compromises for my benefit?' Sunny asked boldly. 'You see, you expect me to do all the compromising. When I'm difficult, it's like a chess game with you in which you make moves to corner me.'

Raj elevated an ebony brow. 'A little dramatic…?'

'No, I'm not being dramatic!' Sunny shot back at him, her hands on her hips. 'You make everything sound so logical! The clothes, the stupid diamond, the nanny! But I don't want to change and I don't want to move house either.'

'Do you want me?' Raj asked with lethal composure. 'Let's face it, it all comes down to how much you want me. I've already changed my habits and routine for you, which is something I've never done for a woman before. This is all new for me as well. So, you don't wish to move house? If I accept that, how could I ever visit you in your current home? Where would my security team stay? How would they guard the property?'

Sunny threw up a silencing hand. 'Don't say anything more!' she gasped, stricken.

'Are you aware that Pansy, as my niece, should have a bodyguard as well?' Raj continued inexorably. 'And what about you, since you have conceived my child? Don't you realise that your security in your little rural nest could be targeted by people who would want to access my money through you? Those are harsh truths, Sunny. They may not be what you want to hear but they are reality all the same.'

Sunny had turned bone white as he spelled out those hard facts. No, she hadn't thought about security needs for any of them. But Raj had said something that had cut her in two and made it almost impossible to maintain her concentration.

Do you want me? Let's face it, it all comes down to how much you want me.

She wanted him way too much for her own peace

of mind. Way too much for sanity. He already had her craving him like an addictive drug. It was too much, the way she was feeling was *too much*. All her emotions were jangling inside her and rising up in a flood from a tumultuous base.

She breathed in deep, pale and stiff as board. 'I think we should break up.'

'We're not travelling in that direction. We haven't been together long enough for you to make a logical decision on that score,' Raj decreed without hesitation.

'You can't tell me what I can and cannot do,' Sunny flung at him angrily.

'I'm not trying to do that. I'm asking you to take a deep breath and calm down.'

'Calm down? Isn't that what men always say when a woman disagrees with them?' Sunny flared, trying to thrust him out of her path to enable her to open the door behind him.

He was too big and he was as solid as a rock but once she'd registered her intent he flung up his expressive hands in exasperation and stepped out of her path. 'Think about this. Think about what you're doing and why.'

Sunny yanked open the door with positive violence and scrutinised him with fierce violet-blue eyes. 'You're dumped.'

'Seriously?' Raj elevated another expressive black brow as if she were throwing a strop about nothing.

'Just because it hasn't happened to you before

doesn't mean it can't happen,' Sunny hissed and, marching back from the door, she scooped up the property file and walked back to plant it into his reluctant arms.

'Adults talk problems through, sort things out,' Raj informed her.

And she wanted to hit him. The violence coursing through her terrified her. She had a mental image of pushing him out of the door and pushing until he fell down the stairs. And then that image crumpled at the picture of him being physically hurt because that was more than she could bear in the highly emotional mood she was in. No, she didn't want to hurt him, she wanted to shut him up, bounce him out of his inhuman calm and control and make him leave.

'We can't be sorted. We're a hellish mess together.'

'We could do better than this,' Raj conceded with pronounced reluctance. 'It's a question of cooperation. Why are you so angry with me?'

Sunny gritted her teeth. 'You're trying to move me into one of your mansions!'

'Some women would be reasonably happy about that,' Raj dared to declare.

'I'm not!' she almost shrieked at him in her ire, scared of listening or believing lest he begin to talk her round.

'I could buy up all the land round you and extend your house,' Raj remarked. 'You see, I can compromise in a sensible way, but, admittedly, only when

I'm forced. I am a challenging character. I acknowledge that.'

'You didn't even allow me the freedom to speak
to your guests this evening!' Sunny accused, heading off on a new tack.

'My guests were too curious about you and I didn't
want you to put yourself in a position where you
might drop too many private facts, which could later
cause you embarrassment or hurt. You are very innocent and trusting with the people that you meet.
I admire that quality in you. But it makes you very
vulnerable. You take an optimistic view of life, a
view that is directly opposed to my own. I am more
cynical, and my motivation this evening was to look
after you, not to clip your wings or to stifle your natural friendliness.'

'Don't talk down to me! Go back to your own
room,' Sunny hurled at him, because she already
knew that Raj could undoubtedly reason himself out
of anything short of murder.

'We'll talk tomorrow,' Raj breathed with finality,
and he walked out, shoulders squared, back straight
as a board.

No, they wouldn't be talking tomorrow, Sunny decided fiercely. She would leave at the crack of dawn,
go home, move on with her life, rediscover the plea-
sures she had neglected since Raj had entered her life
and thrown everything up in the air. Of course, she
would still have to maintain his connection to Pansy
and make those visits every month. And eventually

the baby would presumably enter that arrangement as well, she thought abstractedly. For the first time, he had referred to the baby other than as a 'development'. And he had referred to the baby as being *his* child. Well, her baby wasn't his child, it was *hers*.

Every just bone in her body was jarred by that unkind thought and she winced for herself and got ready for bed. But some of what Raj had told her about their *security* needs lingered heavily with her. Were she, Pansy and their unborn child at risk because of their connection to the richest man in the world? Why had she not foreseen that danger for herself? Why had she been so blind about that harsh reality? Raj was right, she didn't like stuff of that nature, always shut out such frightening possibilities. Guilt folded round her that she had forced Raj to spell out the obvious. Suddenly she was appreciating that she had never been in full control of her relationship with Raj, nor would she ever be. Not when their baby's very safety could be compromised by some ghastly threat.

Seriously shaken by such thoughts but unable to see what she could possibly do to remedy the situation other than distance them all from Raj, she set her alarm for an ungodly early hour. Life without Raj, life without the excitement and the host of other responses he sparked in her. For goodness' sake, she had been on her own and perfectly happy that way for years and she would be again, she promised herself. She would bury herself in her work. She would have *two* children to raise. She still had the house to finish. Exhaustion finally plunged her into sleep.

CHAPTER NINE

GALES OF LAUGHTER greeted Sunny before she even made it into Pansy's bedroom.

It was five-thirty in the morning and faint purple shadows lay like fading bruises below Sunny's eyes. She had put on more make-up than usual because she felt like a mess and the sight of Raj down on the floor playing with their niece, who was still clad in her pyjamas, was the last thing she needed in the mood she was in. She had been hoping to leave his home without seeing him again.

Stunning dark golden eyes sought out her evasive gaze with determination. 'I wanted to see her before you left. She hasn't had her breakfast yet. Maria helped me change her…er nappy. Pansy thought that was very funny because I was fumbling and slow and she kicked me while I was trying to work out the tapes.'

'This is the best time of the day for her. She's always full of joy and nonsense,' Sunny told him unevenly, bending down to lift her niece, who had come running with a smile as soon as she'd appeared.

Pansy gave her a noisy kiss and then indicated that she wanted to get down again and return to playing with Raj.

Raj was down on the floor, sheathed in faded jeans and a T-shirt, the casual attire not screening an inch of his glorious long muscular frame. He had lined up little cars for Pansy to rearrange. 'I thought she would only like girl things but she brought the cars to me.'

'She changes her mind from one day to the next. She plays with everything. I'll get her breakfast now and…I suppose, see you next month, however we organise it,' she muttered, desperate to escape because he looked so natural down there on the floor with Pansy.

So natural and so very handsome with his high, sharply defined cheekbones, sculpted lips and hard masculine jawline, not to mention the lean, powerful body clearly defined by well-worn denim. He'd been correct when he had said he had changed, he *had* adapted. The guy she had first met in his designer suit would not have put himself forward in the same way, would not have worked at interacting with a toddler, would not have overcome his own misgivings and awkwardness to such an extent. And she respected him for the huge effort he had made and knew that she would never do anything to undermine his relationship with Pansy.

After all, he was still the man she loved, still the male she had dumped in a clumsy effort to get her own life back…only to finally register that perhaps getting her own life back would never be possible.

'I'm sorry,' she said abruptly. 'I'm sorry for some of what I said. 'I know your intentions were good.'

'Don't doubt that,' he told her with assurance. 'You need space to think.'

No, she thought ferociously, she didn't need space to think, she needed to work out how to raise a defensive resistance, how to remain pleasant and friendly without intimacy. It was no help to have Raj there on the floor in front of her, displaying all the characteristics that she found irresistible. That quick and clever mind, that cool inescapable grasp of logic in control. And then there was the long, sleek, utterly sensual length of him, able to offer so much amazing pleasure, that pleasure, that excitement that she had never known before and therefore was so much more vulnerable to receiving.

She craved him in the most basic ways and that was a wake-up call for her to be on her guard, not to settle for superficial stuff but to hold on hard to her defences. Raj had made her crave sex. Just acknowledging that embarrassed her in his radius. Here she was, a victim of a weakness that she had never dreamt even existed. She might have ditched him but she still wanted him.

Raj departed and she got Pansy dressed for breakfast and took her downstairs but still the recollection of Raj lingered. Raj *trying*, Raj *adapting*, Raj proving that he could change, just as she *could* change, she reminded herself ruefully.

Sunny was climbing into her car, ready to leave, when Raj appeared at her window. She lowered it, mindful of a desire not to behave as though she was running away like a coward. He gazed down at her, dark as night eyes brooding, and it was so sexy that her toes curled in response. He had amazingly long lashes, amazingly penetrating dark eyes. Wake up, girl, she urged herself, striving to escape from the charismatic spell he cast.

'So, see you next month,' she said brightly, feeling like an idiot.

'Any doctor's appointments that I need to know about?' Raj enquired perfectly politely.

'Well, yes, my first ultrasound,' she confided reluctantly. 'In a couple of weeks.'

'I won't want to miss that,' Raj assured her.

'But we never talked about this…about the exact level of your involvement…if any,' she reminded him.

'Be fair. You wouldn't *let* me,' he pointed out quietly.

'I'll send you the date,' she proffered thinly, because stepping away from the intimacy, setting herself free from her longing for Raj meant going cold turkey and decreasing any closer connections.

'Don't try to shut me out,' he breathed with sudden urgency. 'This is my first child. This is *very* exciting for me.'

And she thought of that admission the whole drive home.

Exciting for me.

No, she hadn't expected that from Raj. Something so basic and yet, so life-changing, she acknowledged ruefully. Of course, he was curious. Of course, he was excited. This would be his *first* child. Pansy had softened him up, made him aware of children in so many basic ways, and now he was ready for that challenge. And she? She had tried to shut him out, without intending that, without meaning to do that to him. She had leapfrogged over all the reasons that he couldn't cut her off to pretend as though none of those things was happening.

She hadn't allowed him to talk about his feelings about the baby she had conceived. She had denied him that outlet. My word, she had been selfish, trying to shut him out from what would soon be as much his business as hers. And all so that she could redraw her boundaries for his benefit to keep him at a distance. My baby, *not* yours, my child, *none* of your business.

She had behaved badly. She had forced him into a corner by making her own assumptions as to how he would react. Yet the truth was that Raj was not the guy she had assumed he was when they first met. He was a male ever willing to grow and move on to fresh territory. Her brain could not handle that conundrum when she was so very aware that she had ditched him.

* * *

A week later, Sunny wakened to the dogs barking and Pansy crying. Wondering weakly if she could have slept in, she rolled out of bed. Her mobile phone was ringing and the doorbell was buzzing and both at the same time. Grabbing up her robe with her brow furrowed, she hurried off to deal with Pansy first.

Through the glazed front door she saw dark shadows suggesting that more than one person was crowded on her doorstep. She sped into Pansy's room to retrieve her niece. The toddler hugged close, she returned to her bedroom to answer the phone. It was Gemma.

'Sunny? I had a journalist on my doorstep yesterday asking questions about you. I sent him about his business but my neighbour told me that there's an article about you in the paper today. I'm bringing it round. It's a lot of drivel!'

Conscious of the hubbub round her front door and that people with cameras were trying to look in through her windows, Sunny retreated to the kitchen to let the dogs out. She lifted her mobile to answer it when it rang again. Raj's cool, level voice greeted her.

'I've sent help to keep the crowd of paparazzi in control…and I'll drop in later in person. Don't read the newspapers for a day or two,' Raj advised.

A knock sounded on the back door. Then it opened a mere few inches. 'Miss Barker? Mr Belanger sent me with my team. I'm Sam and we're clearing the paps from your garden back onto the road where the police will handle them if they obstruct the flow of traffic. I suggest you let the dogs back indoors again. I had to detach the little one from a man's ankle.' Bert was handed through the ajar door, little round eyes huge at the indignity, spindly legs pedalling frantically in mid-air. 'He's ferocious, isn't he?'

'Sometimes,' Sunny conceded, because Bert could also be very cuddly, but she really didn't care if he'd frightened off any unwanted intruders with cameras. As she grabbed Bert, Bear squeezed past Sam into the kitchen and sat down, relieved, it seemed, to be away from all the noise and fuss.

In twenty minutes, Sunny had changed and dressed Pansy, and contrived to freshen up in the bathroom. Then she fed the dogs, put on the kettle and gave Pansy her breakfast. By that time, Gemma was at the back door.

'My word, there's a huge number of journalists out on the road. A policeman was trying to move them on and then there are...*private* security people here helping out?' she queried in fascination. 'All suited and wearing sunglasses and those earpieces, looking like they belong in a James Bond movie.'

'They're courtesy of Raj,' Sunny confided breathlessly.

Gemma was surprised. 'But I thought that was over.'

'Evidently he'll still look out for our welfare,' Sunny said with a slight shrug.

Gemma spread a crumpled tabloid newspaper on

the table. There were far more photos of Christabel than there were of Sunny. But then her late half-sister had been both glamorous and well known. In fact there was only one photo of Sunny, depicting her by Raj's side at the fund-raising event at Ashton Hall. She could have done, however, without reviewing photos of Christabel falling out of various nightclubs, obviously under the weather, and she certainly would have preferred not to see the scene of the car crash again that had taken her half-sister and brother-in-law's lives.

'They're trying to insinuate that you're a druggie too.'

'No, I think they were short of dirt to serve up, so they rehashed poor Christabel's worst moments instead. My only public profile is as an artist and you can't get much mileage out of that.'

'They're madly speculating about you and Raj… and, er, *that* diamond.'

'It was on loan. Raj did warn me that there'd be a lot of speculation.'

'Apparently, he's never shown off an actual girlfriend before and they're wondering if it's just a family connection linked to Pansy or something *more*,' Gemma proffered as Sunny speed-read through the article, catching the use of certain words to describe her that suggested she might be a little weird with her penchant for long skirts, animals and wild foraging.

'So, they know about Pansy.' Sunny sighed. 'That won't please Raj.'

'The press have probably always known about her. They just weren't interested in the poor child until you came along and developed a bond with her uncle.'

'Unca,' Pansy said on cue.

'Uncle,' Sunny corrected.

Pansy went off into her 'nose...eye...mouth' spiel.

'Look, I'll clear off now. I know you have that painting to finish. Do you want me to take the dogs with me?'

'Thanks, but there's no need while I'm here.' Sunny saw the older woman to the back door and recommended that she use the shortcut across the paddock to avoid the men with cameras.

She finished her painting while Pansy was enjoying a nap, and was getting cleaned up when she heard a helicopter overhead. She had put on a green sundress although in the autumnal cool it was a little chilly for it, but it still fitted her when so many other items had become too tight. When she heard the helicopter coming in to land, she ran outside, paused a moment to soothe Muffy, who was shifting anxiously in her stall, and then walked on out to see Raj arriving. A bunch of security men fanned out in a circle round the craft and then Raj sprang out, black hair ruffling in the breeze and so vital and so intensely masculine that she clenched her teeth together on a visceral inner tightening that had nothing to do with nerves and everything to do with desire.

He strode towards her, effortlessly elegant in a

mid-grey designer suit that faithfully outlined his broad shoulders, lean hips and long powerful legs to the manner born. He looked amazing and utterly out of place in a paddock. He was metropolitan fashionable and immaculate and even as she watched cameras were lifting above the boundary hedge to catch photos of his arrival and she winced.

Raj ignored the cameras but several of his security team went running in their direction.

'You didn't need to come all this way.'

'A slight detour. I'm on my way back from Scotland. It wasn't a problem,' he countered, striding ahead of her to thrust open the back door into the kitchen. 'How are you managing all this? Have the paps been annoying you much?'

'Not with your security men keeping them away from the windows and out of the garden,' she fielded lightly. 'In fact, I actually finished my painting this morning.'

'You'll have to let me see it.' Raj sank down at the kitchen table right in front of the newspaper she had intended to cram into the recycling bin. 'I see you didn't take my advice… I can't say that surprises me.'

'Coffee?' she prompted, keen to change the subject.

Raj assented with a nod but he was too busy scrutinising the article to look back at her. In any case, she was still in his mind's eye, all soft and flowy in a simple green dress, relaxed, casual, golden hair a little rumpled. She was sort of squinting at him too, which meant that she hadn't got her contact lenses in and probably had mislaid her spectacles again. There was a tiny streak of yellow paint above her brow. He breathed in deep and slow and strove to study the newsprint instead.

'I hate the way they've associated you with Christabel. I shouldn't say it, but she was very bad news for Ethan. He was a grown man but he was easily led. He liked anything that got him high and she was much the same and when the other men came into the picture, it was almost impossible to keep him steady and sober. I tried to get him into rehab but Christabel wouldn't have it, said I had no right to interfere. And she was right, but their child was there by then and someone had to speak up and try to make a judgement call.'

Sunny had paused in making the coffee to stare at him. 'Christabel had other men?' she murmured in shock.

'I'm sorry. I assumed you would know. She wasn't exactly secretive or discreet about it. Ethan wasn't enough for her and her acting career had crashed because of the drugs. She craved attention and her lovers gave her that. I should've got him out of the marriage, but he still loved her. I could've bought her off. If I had, Ethan would still be alive…they both might be. I failed him.' Raj's dark eyes were bleak with pain and regret and her heart went out to him. 'He needed a save but I was the wrong person to help. He resented me, so I stepped back.'

'I'm so sorry, Raj. I totally misunderstood the situation when I accused you of spoiling him by indulging him,' she whispered gruffly.

'My mother did the spoiling. Ethan was the centre of her world and when she died, he went to pieces. I had to pick up those pieces and he hated that too.'

'And where were you when all this spoiling was happening?' she asked curiously.

'Studying at one or another university, winning prizes and newspaper column inches, setting up my first companies. I didn't see much of either of them growing up, so I didn't have the chance to develop a normal sibling relationship with Ethan.'

'Someone has to be willing to accept help to *be* helped,' she mused reflectively. 'Sometimes all you can do is stand back and mind your own business. There's nothing in that newspaper article that upset me, other than the writer choosing to rehash Christabel's most public mistakes.'

'The press won't leave you alone now. That's *my* fault too. I shouldn't have shown you off at the fundraiser at Ashton.'

'You probably shouldn't have come here to see me either. That will only incite more rumours.' Sunny sighed.

Raj pushed back the chair, his lean, strong face taut. 'I won't let that keep me away from you. I want you and Pansy and the baby in my life. Surely you can understand that?'

The super-gifted male with everything had never had a proper family and quite naturally he now wanted what he had never had.

'I do understand it,' she conceded quietly.

The silent tension between them smouldered. Sunny looked away first just as Bear roamed a little too close to Bert's basket and Bert leapt out and began to bark in a passion at the larger dog.

Raj stood up. 'Stop it!' he thundered down at the chihuahua.

Bert's big round eyes bulged and he fell silent. Then he turned in his tracks and raced back into his basket.

'He only needs a firm word.'

'From a man, I suspect. His late owner was a man. Certainly, Bert doesn't listen to me like that.' Sunny viewed the little dog curled up in his basket as if he would not dream of hurling a rude challenge at another animal. He was perfectly calm.

Raj studied her with veiled eyes. They had a problem, a major problem, and he wasn't even sure that she recognised the fact. Sunny was too busy trying to stay in control of everything, including him…had he been the sort of guy willing to accept that. He believed that, fortunately for all of them, he was *not* that guy. Look at the chaos she had already created with her determined attempt to keep him out of their lives! But, if they married, he would have all three of them under his protection. Sunny, Pansy, his child.

That was what needed to happen. That would fix the situation, he decided with cold logic.

'Sunny…' Raj breathed without warning. 'Marry me.'

Sunny blinked and stared incredulously back at him. 'Raj—'

'I mean it. I don't want the three of you on a sporadic visiting basis. I want you all permanently. Marriage is the logical next step forward for us and it will overcome many of the irritations currently making your life difficult. If you're my wife, I can shield you from all such annoyances. I will not have you depicted in the press as some temporary occupant in my bed, a target for insinuation and rumour. Nor do I want my child becoming a target.'

He closed his hands over hers and tugged her closer.

'You've shocked me,' she whispered truthfully, shaking her head as if to clear it of the mental fog that had engulfed her. 'I really wasn't expecting this.'

A big hand rested against her breast. 'Your heart's racing.'

Sunny tensed, wanting his fingers to stroke, cup, caress, colour flaring in her cheeks. 'It's not every day I get a marriage proposal. In fact, this is my very first.'

'So, say yes,' Raj husked softly.

'And you'll promise not to be bossy and overprotective any more?'

'I don't think you'd credit that kind of promise from me.'

The doorbell was buzzing again and she backed away with a sigh. 'That must be a real visitor,' she assumed. 'Or your security wouldn't have let them past the gate.'

She walked out to the hall and opened the front door and was completely disconcerted to find Jack Henderson on the step. Jack smiled warmly at her, something he hadn't done in her vicinity since their breakup as teenagers. 'Jack?' she whispered questioningly.

'I was worried about you in the midst of all this newspaper madness. It's not you. You like a quiet life.'

'I do, but Raj is here and I'll be fine. The fuss will die down.'

'Raj Belanger, right?' Jack checked, his mouth twisting. 'Pansy's uncle?'

'That's correct.'

'As soon as he leaves, you'll be all right.'

A strong arm closed round her taut figure from the back. 'Sunny will be leaving *with* me,' Raj decreed.

Her lashes fluttered in bewilderment. 'But—'

'When I'm here, Sunny doesn't have to worry about anything,' Raj delivered with precision. 'Thank you for the thought but she is not in need of assistance. Unlike you, I would never abandon her when life gets rough.'

Paling at that derisive challenge, Jack turned on his heel and walked back down the path.

Sunny was aghast. She twisted her head. 'How the heck could you say that to him?'

'Easily. He ran out on you when you needed support. I would never do that to you.'

CHAPTER TEN

SUNNY FOLDED HER ARMS. 'So, according to you, I'm leaving here *with* you.'

Raj shrugged a broad shoulder. 'You haven't given me an answer yet to my proposal.'

Sunny was thinking about being married to Raj. The prospect made her feel quite dizzy when what she really needed to do was to keep her feet on the ground and her brain at full functioning capacity. 'There would have to be negotiation.'

'Of course. Conditions?'

'You would have to travel less and choose one property as a family base for the sake of the children.'

'Children,' Raj stressed. 'Not a feature of life I ever expected to experience. And then you came along.'

'Yes, I came along and being with me will entail certain adjustments in your lifestyle. Children need a home and stability,' Sunny declared. 'You can't continue to flit from one property to another because children need to attend schools and enjoy recreational activities. Not only do they need a routine to thrive, they also need to socialise with other children. None of that can be achieved with a father who expects them to travel with him and who flies somewhere virtually every day.'

'Not every day,' Raj qualified with a frown. 'We'll use my London base as a home but there will be times when travel is unavoidable.'

Sunny gazed back at him. The prospect of a father for Pansy and her unborn child was a huge draw but the prospect of simply having constant access to the man she loved was the more powerful attraction.

'I appreciate that this is not romantic in the least,' Raj conceded wryly as he tugged her up against him with a gruff sound deep in his chest that reverberated through her slighter, smaller frame like a wake-up call of sensual response. He pushed her hair back from her face and claimed her soft lips with hungry, driving intensity and she shivered against him, insanely conscious of the long hard thrust of his erection and the dampness between her legs.

'That doesn't matter,' she muttered. 'You can't do romantic if you can't do love.'

'And I'm definitely not likely to be doing that,' Raj drawled impatiently.

'I just want you,' she said truthfully. 'And I want to be happy. How is this massive change in our lives going to work?'

'The good news is…you just leave it all to me. Pack what you need for twenty-four hours and everything else will be transported to you tomorrow,' Raj told her. 'Muffy can go to Ashton Hall and the dogs and the cat, of course, can be with us by this evening.'

Breathless at those ideas, Sunny whispered apologetically, 'And there's ducks down by the pond in the bottom corner of the paddock.'

Raj breathed in deep. 'Not a problem,' he declared. 'Now go and pack while I make the arrangements.'

Sunny hovered in the doorway. 'Where will we get married?'

'Ashton. It's licensed for ceremonies.'

'Could the vicar at my church do the honours? And I've friends and neighbours here who I'd like to invite,' she said quietly.

'Of course.'

Sunny stayed in the doorway. 'You shouldn't have blamed Jack for the way he treated me. He was only seventeen at the time, as was I.'

'He made you feel defective,' Raj contradicted. 'He wanted perfect and you don't get perfect in this life. He was cruel and he had years in which to think better of his treatment of you and offer his regrets. But he never *did*, did he?'

Her eyes dropped from his as she reflected on how much it would have meant to her had Jack thought better of his comments at the time. 'No, you're right, he didn't.'

'Rest assured that I will never ever expect perfect, but I will not allow those who hurt you to go unpunished,' he extended grimly. 'You're too soft, too forgiving, but that balances out my more cynical, harsh nature.'

'I'll go and pack. What about this house?'

'You've got plenty of time to decide what you want to do with it. Relax.'

'I need to organise the delivery of that painting,' she muttered distractedly. 'And no, you don't need to take charge of that too!'

'It might be easier if you put your specs on,' Raj suggested, filching the pair he had noticed abandoned beside the sink and extending them to her.

'I don't know how I ever managed without you,' Sunny framed abstractedly.

'There's a streak of paint above your left eyebrow,' Raj added helpfully. 'And you were going to pack.'

Several hours later, Sunny and Pansy landed with Raj at his London home. There had been some frantic packing. Deprived of Sunny's full attention, Pansy had thrown her first tantrum. There had been a whole lot of wailing and sobbing. Neither food nor attention had consoled her and eventually she had fallen asleep nestled close to Bear, who had been very troubled by her distress. Raj had carried his niece onto the helicopter with all the delicacy of a cat burglar, terrified of her waking up again mid-air. But, exhausted by her shenanigans, the little girl had slept and wakened to Maria's familiar face and a nursery full of toys.

Sunny, however, was greeted in the ballroom by a stylist and a wedding planner. An endless parade of models on a hastily set-up catwalk displayed wedding dresses for her examination. And she fell in love on the spot with the one that had delicate flowers embroidered all over it, of course she did. It was sleeveless and it had a detachable train, a lowish laced back and a modest tailored corset bodice that would give her all the support she required.

Careful measurements were taken. A second dress was suggested for the reception. Sunny chose a sleek elegant gown with cap sleeves and a flattering neckline that she planned to wear with comfortable ballet slippers. She spoke to the stylist about a toning wedding outfit for Pansy and then the stylist moved on to footwear. While Sunny was deliberating on the temptation of pearlised very high-heeled shoes and more traditional diamanté-encrusted sandals, Raj joined them.

'The doctor will be here in an hour.'

'What doctor?' she asked, wandering away from the fashion crew around her for some privacy.

'The obstetrician I arranged to call here this evening to see us. He'll give you your first ultrasound as I won't be in the UK next week for the one you mentioned.'

Sunny stared at him in a daze. 'That's a lot to unpack.'

'I'm trying to be helpful.' Raj had the nerve to look reproachful. 'I didn't want to miss out on the ultrasound and I want you to be checked over just to be sure everything's in order.'

'Where are you flying away to?' In spite of her at-

tempt to make that a normal question she could hear
the slight accusing note in her own voice.

'New York…and possibly, er, a little stopover in
Iceland. I'll be away ten days but back in time for the
wedding. I've put staff at your disposal and everyone knows you're in charge here,' Raj informed her
with satisfaction. 'I have to clear the decks to get
some time off to spend with you after the wedding.'

Sunny nodded, not wishing to be a nag. 'When
do you leave?'

'In a couple of hours…late flight.'

She gritted her teeth. 'Yet you took me away from
home.'

'By tomorrow, all your belongings will be here
and you can go on just as you would at your former
home.' Closing one hand over hers, he urged her back
out into the hall, where they were free of an audi-
ence. 'This is for you…'

Lifting her hand, he threaded a diamond ring onto
her wedding finger. It had the same blue depth as
the stone in the pendant and it was equally magnificent. 'It's gorgeous,' she conceded. 'But I wanted to
be with you tonight.'

Raj frowned. 'I thought being free after the wedding was more important. I'm not used to consulting anyone about my decisions. I accept that that will
have to change to some extent.'

With determination, Sunny laced her beringed
hand with his long clenching fingers. 'It's not a problem. But I'll miss you.'

And he grabbed her up into a passionate kiss that sent the blood drumming like mad through her veins. 'I will miss you too.'

Sunny drifted back into the ballroom to rejoin the fashion crew and make selections. Her lips were tingling from the urgency of his and her breasts were tight and her breathing uneven. She had been looking forward to a wickedly rapturous reunion and then he'd told her that he was leaving her for ten days. And that was Raj, along with the unexpected gift of a superb engagement ring and a medical check-up. Suddenly she was laughing at the sheer unexpectedness of his energetic, driven temperament, the speed with which he operated, the many levels on which he thought and planned in advance. Naturally, with all that complexity and no habit of discussing plans with others, he was bound to trip up occasionally.

There was a lot more wedding planning to be done, from the colour of the tableware to the cake to the music—already organised, she was told—and the number of guests. Hundreds, she was informed, and that was even before she added her own list of people to the invitations. For the first time, it occurred to her that she was going to be the bride in a massive showpiece of a wedding. A pregnant bride. But people didn't really worry about that these days, she reminded herself, although undoubtedly there would be some who would suspect that Raj was marrying her only because of the baby.

Only Sunny would not be one of those people. Raj

wanted her and he wanted Pansy as well. She had realised that truth very quickly. He was keen to claim
the family that he had never had. It was a choice he
had never enjoyed before. Marrying her, she appreciated, would be something akin to a science experiment for Raj. He was greeting the opportunity with
enthusiasm but would still be waiting to see how the
chips fell. She and Pansy and her animals would be
on trial, she decided ruefully. Ultimately, Raj would
have to decide whether they added to or detracted
from his untrammelled life of not committing to anything other than business. It was a grave, sobering
thought to cherish before a wedding.

The obstetrician, who arrived after the fashion
team had departed, was suave and charming, vis-
ibly tickled pink to be invited to take care of her
pregnancy. With him came his nurse and a technician and a lot of medical equipment. Raj looked on
the cavalcade with approbation.

'I want to know that you're safe, that I've taken
every possible precaution with your health,' he confided.

She could not be critical of such an outlook. Yes,
it annoyed her that he had gone above her head and
yet, on the other hand, she was delighted that he was
sufficiently interested in seeing their unborn child to
arrange an ultrasound that he too could be present to
enjoy. Ushered into a private reception room with a
doctor, she had a comprehensive medical question-
naire to fill in and all the usual tests.

Raj joined them for a discussion of how her previous reproductive problems might play out during her current pregnancy. Raj's troubled brow cleared when the obstetrician confessed that he saw no reason for her past surgical history to influence her pregnancy in any way. Then it was time for her to lie down on the couch and the technician moved forward and the gel was rubbed over her slightly protuberant tummy.

'I'm not flat any more,' she sighed.

'That's my baby in there. You don't need to make excuses on that score,' Raj proclaimed with satisfaction.

'Would you like to know the gender? It may be possible to see now but it may also not be possible,' they were warned. 'It depends on the position of the baby in the uterus.'

The screen before them came alive and at first Sunny couldn't pick out anything but lighter spaces and darker places. Then the technician was talking them through it and she saw the tiny legs and the little arms and her heart was in her mouth and Raj was leaning forward with pronounced interest to learn that they could look forward to becoming the parents of a baby boy.

Raj closed her hand into his and grinned at her, delighted and not even trying to hide the fact. 'A boy?'

'A large boy. Miss Barker is already showing more pregnant than would have been expected at present. It's possible that a C-section may be necessary at the delivery stage, but we'll know more about that in a few months,' the obstetrician told them with as-surance. 'There is no cause for concern at this time. Miss Barker is in good health, as is the baby.'

A wide smile on his sculpted lips, Raj rose from his seat and helped her off the couch as she righted her clothing. He said all that was polite, checked that a further visit was scheduled and guided Sunny back out again. 'That was…unexpectedly *very* exciting,' he admitted in evident surprise. 'Our baby, there on screen for us to see. A kind of first hello. Amazing!'

'You've never seen an ultrasound before?'

'Why would I have? I know how the tech works but I was never interested. I didn't believe that I would ever have a child. It has never been one of my goals,' Raj admitted quietly. 'But now that our son is on the way? It's changed everything. You have en-riched my life, Sunny. I can never thank you enough for that.'

Sunny paled, wishing that he had used his words in another way. As it was, she felt as though he was more excited about their child than he was about mar-rying her. And how could she be happy about that? After all, any woman could have given him a child and that ability did not make her either special or unique. She had lucked out in more ways than one, she thought unhappily. She had fallen accidentally pregnant by a very rich guy, who was thoroughly enjoying the experience even of her actually *being* pregnant with *his* child. But it wasn't personal. It wasn't love and maybe it was naïve of her to still

want more than the romantic trappings of an engagement ring and a free hand to organise the society
wedding of the year.

Raj was rich and intelligent. He wouldn't marry
her in any hole-and-corner way that might suggest
that he was marrying her unwillingly or only because she carried his child. No, Raj would push the
boat out in public. He would also look after every
aspect of her pregnancy and guard her from every
ill to ensure her health and security. He would do all
of that for his child…not for her in person. Her baby
had somehow become more important than she was,
she conceded heavily.

A little voice in her troubled brain cried out that
Raj had given up his convenient mistresses for her
benefit and that at that point he had had no idea that
it was even possible for her to conceive. But that
was sex, she reminded herself. When she had said
no to Raj initially, his interest in her had grown exponentially. She had then become infinitely more
desirable in her unattainability because he, primar-
ily, was not accustomed to women saying no to him.
Her conception had been a massive surprise, but it
was also something new and fresh and Raj Belanger
was intellectually programmed to be fascinated by
anything new and fresh. Furthermore, his attitude
to children had been tempered by his meetings with
Pansy. Pansy had gently eased him into the idea of
a paternal role.

'You're very quiet,' Raj remarked. 'I have to leave.'

'I can cope,' she said brightly, forcing a smile as Bear and Bert surged across the big hall to greet her.

Bert, however, raced straight past her to gambol round Raj's feet. 'Why's he doing that?' he demanded, stepping back in surprise from the little dog's approach.

'Evidently, he's *your* dog now. It's pretty obvious he prefers men and I'm the lady who tried and failed to rehome him with two different women, so Bert has finally found his new owner and you're stuck with him.'

'But he's an insane bully.'

'Not around you, he's not. He *listens* to you.'

'The cat doesn't. When I told him off for scratching at my desk, he stuck his nose in the air and strolled away.'

'We should've packed the log.'

'He has a scratching post.'

'He likes his log. Don't you think I tried a scratching post for him? He's choosy.'

'I'll phone you first thing in the morning when I'm in New York,' Raj promised. 'And try to do some shopping for our honeymoon. You'll need lighter clothing.'

'Where are we going?'

'Haven't quite decided yet but there'll be sunshine and plants for you to be inspired by,' he said confidently.

The next ten days were packed tight with activity for Sunny. She had innumerable calls from friends, astonished by their wedding invitations and the identity of the man she was to marry. Only a few of them had seen that photograph of her with Raj in the newspaper but, as public knowledge of their wedding plans spread, there were a couple of articles printed about her in more serious newspapers with references to her career as a botanical artist. Mid-week, the social worker in charge of Pansy's case sent her documents to enable Raj to become part of the adoption application. And Sunny moved to Ashton Hall to get ready for the wedding.

Raj phoned her every day until he reached Iceland and that was the last she heard from him. When he had still not returned the night before the ceremony, Sunny started getting antsy. He didn't answer his phone either. The morning of the wedding she enjoyed the attentions of a make-up artist and a hairstylist but her nerves were torn by Raj's continuing absence. Surely he wouldn't jilt her at the altar? If something were truly wrong, she told herself, it probably would have been in the newspapers or someone would have contacted her, wouldn't they?

News of his late arrival was brought by her hairstylist, who reached the hall at about the same time. Relief spread through Sunny. Attired in her gown, she descended the stairs, confident of the fact that she had never taken so much care with her appearance and that she looked her very best.

Raj watched his bride move towards him. She had never looked more beautiful than in her fairy-tale dress with its tiny beaded flowers, the diamond pendant at her throat, a simple coronet crowning her upswept hair. A tremulous smile softened her tense lips when she saw him. He gave her the bunch of simple wildflowers to carry and took her hand in his to walk her into the ballroom through their assembled guests.

'I thought you weren't going to make it,' she said breathlessly, striving to look neither to the left nor to the right at the sheer mass of people watching them. In any case, she was still reliving that first glimpse of Raj, his tall, lean, powerful frame sheathed in a morning suit of exquisite tailoring. Black hair tousled by his ever-restless fingers, stunning dark golden eyes locked to her, his strong bronzed features taut. Gorgeous, drop-dead gorgeous, and to be all hers now.

'Mechanical problems with the jet we were in, an accident in a cave with a foolhardy friend, who had to be rescued, had to reorganise our transport, smashed my phone into a wall. *Dire*,' he admitted feelingly in a measured undertone and staring out of a tall window into the sky where a faint distant whine advertised the presence of the tiny craft darting above the house. 'Those blasted press drones chasing pictures,' he added. 'It's illegal to jam them. I'd shoot them out of the sky if I could but that's not legal either.'

'Forget about them,' Sunny advised.

Her fine brows rose as they arrived with the vicar at the altar set up for the ceremony. A *cave*? What on earth had he been doing in a cave of all things? But the marriage service had begun and it was the old-style version. She was absorbed, making her vows, listening with intense amusement as Raj's innate impatience had him diving in too early with his responses. Finally they exchanged wedding rings.

Raj skimmed a brief kiss over her mouth, evidently no fan of public displays and mindful of her make-up, and she wanted to grab him by the lapels and demand that he kiss her properly, an urge that mortified her. It was done. They were married, and as that intoxicating awareness infiltrated her she was shot back to reality by Pansy finally breaking free from Maria's restraining hold and darting over to her to grab her knees through the dress. Raj swooped down to hoist the little girl up into his arms and she went straight into her 'eyes…nose…mouth' routine.

'It's just like any other day for her.' Sunny chuckled. 'She'll keep us grounded.'

'You look gorgeous in that dress,' Raj told her frankly, dark deep-set eyes caressing.

'Why couldn't you phone me?'

'Because I broke it during the caving accident and everyone else was using theirs.'

'What the heck were you doing in a cave?'

'Stag do. Caving, snow mobiles, white water rafting. Iceland. I enjoyed the first day of it. I like a physical challenge, but when that drunken idiot got hurt fooling around and had to be rescued, I felt as though I was too mature for it all.'

'So, Iceland was a stag do,' she gathered in mounting annoyance, thinking of the way she had been summarily deserted and left to handle all the wedding palaver. 'Is your friend badly hurt?'

'Broken leg and arm. He was lucky to get away that lightly,' Raj advanced.

'You should have mentioned the stag do,' she told him flatly. 'And when you were so late getting here, I thought you might not show up for the wedding, which was very inconsiderate.'

'I'm not used to explaining my every move to anyone!' Raj shot back at her without apology.

Sunny's smile was bleak as they drifted into a drinks reception and many, many congratulatory meetings from their guests. She couldn't match faces to names but she met Raj's closer friends. And all the time she was thinking that, because Raj didn't love her, he was still holding her at a distance. He hadn't shared anything with her. My goodness, had she made a terrible mistake in marrying him?

'I have to get changed for the reception,' Sunny told him, stiff with the effort of keeping up a smile.

'Not before you're photographed in that gown.' Raj signalled the photographer mingling with the crowd and whirled her off.

Thirty minutes of posing was enough for her and she fled upstairs, finding Raj on her heels as she hurried into their bedroom, still seething with anxious thoughts.

'Undo my lacing,' she urged, turning her back on him as she kicked off her high heels and shrank.

The straps slid down her shoulders as the corset loosened. With a husky groan, Raj slid his hands below the bodice to cup her breasts and chafe her straining nipples. An inarticulate cry broke from her lips as she fell back against him and he tugged the dress down so that it fell and bared her for his pleasure. 'Gorgeous,' he said thickly.

'*Raj*—'

'You can say no, although I'll try very hard not to mess up your hair. I'm burning up for you.' He flexed his hips against her bottom and she felt him long and hard and urgent and the warmth in her pelvis heated to boiling point.

'Going to say no,' she framed, out of patience with him. 'Sorry, but no.'

Aware of his dark stare, Sunny climbed into her other dress, sliding her feet into the comfy ballet slippers with relief.

'What's wrong?' Raj demanded.

Sunny rounded on him. 'What's *right*? You're out of touch for days, worrying me, and then you almost miss our wedding… That's how late your arrival was! I was afraid I was being jilted, which is not a thought any bride wants to have. Just because you don't love me, Raj, doesn't mean you can get away with treating me without consideration!'

Raj's lean dark features were rigid. 'That was not my intention. I believed—obviously wrongly—that you had more faith in me than to have such a fear.'

Sunny's heart sank inside her. That stripped their

relationship down to the very barest bones, she thought wretchedly. A male in love would have been more sympathetic towards his bride's feelings but Raj was not in love. Raj had married her to retain access to her and Pansy and eventually his own child. For him, that had been a totally practical solution, neither romantic nor sensitive, and to look for him to show her anything more than a desire for sex was obviously foolish.

When they returned to their guests, the ballroom had been transformed for the reception and they took their seats to be served. There was only one speech, from Raj's best man. Neither of them had relatives to make speeches. While they ate they were entertained by a world-famous female singer. They cut the cake, they danced.

Pansy fell asleep in Sunny's arms. 'Either we stay the night here or we leave soon,' she warned Raj.

'I'll stay for another hour.' Raj dug out his phone. 'You can catch the helicopter with Pansy out to the yacht.'

'I should change,' Sunny said wearily.

'Why bother? You can change when you get there.' He cupped her face with long gentle fingers. 'You look tired and you shouldn't be pushing yourself too hard. It's been a long day.'

A crowd accompanied them outside. Raj helped her board and took charge of his niece to clip her into her seat before climbing back out again. Sunny screened a yawn as she put on the headphones and the helicopter rose in the air.

Raj saw the low-flying drone above first and shouted. His heart leapt into his throat as he watched the drone collide with the rotor blades. The craft lurched and spun as someone screamed and everybody around him backed off, cries of alarm filling the air. Raj felt sick. The helicopter began to drop down and pitched clumsily to one side before the pilot skilfully got it back under control and dropped it somewhat heavily down on the ground again.

Raj was the first to wrench open the doors. He grabbed Sunny, who was wide-eyed and shaking, while someone else released Pansy from her seat. Only a few feet from the craft, he wheeled to an abrupt halt and simply held Sunny. Pale as a sheet, he hugged her close and she realised that he was trembling against her.

'We'll stay the night here,' he breathed. 'I'm not letting you out of my sight again. Excuse me.'

Sunny watched him stride over to speak to the pilot and heard him thank the older man and congratulate him on their safe landing. Maria appeared to retrieve Pansy, who, amazingly, had slumbered through the entire experience.

Raj hovered over a sofa in the drawing room as a doctor checked Sunny out, satisfied that she had merely had a fright and was still in shock. He insisted she stay lying down and Raj crouched down beside her and closed one hand over hers. 'I love you,' he breathed rawly, startling her with that confession and the powerful tenderness lightening his eyes. 'And I only just realised it. How stupid is that?'

Sunny stared up at him with wide rapt eyes. 'I don't get it.'

'If it had been me that had a near-death accident, perhaps you would. I realised that my whole world was in that helicopter and that if it crashed I would lose *everything*—you, Pansy, our baby. It was the most terrifying moment of my life.'

Sunny cupped his jaw with her fingers in dawning wonderment and conviction. 'Seriously?'

'I want to wrap you in a protective cocoon and you wouldn't let me.'

'I knew I was falling in love with you that very first night on the yacht,' she told him softly. 'It was like something in me recognised you very early on. I guessed how you would react to things. You probably don't believe in them, but I think we're soulmates.'

'Soulmates.' Surprisingly, Raj liked that description. She fitted him like the missing piece of a puzzle. He no longer felt alone. He wanted to share stuff with her that he had never wanted to share with anyone. She calmed him when he was on edge, warned him when he was about to go over it. 'You see my flaws, my mistakes, and you still love me?'

'But you're the same with me,' she pointed out tenderly.

'I thought of asking you to marry me the same day that you told me that you were pregnant, but I was scared you would think I was crazy. And then you shut me out and you had the right to do that: your baby, your body.'

'This is your baby too. I was running scared. I didn't want you to think that I was expecting anything from you and I guess I got carried away with my independent speech. Truthfully, I would always have wanted a father for my baby because I didn't really have a father of my own. My father couldn't see past Christabel to see *me*.'

'And I learned how *not* to be a father from mine, who only saw me as a scientific subject for a study that might make him famous. When you first told me you had conceived, I was terrified because I didn't think I would know *how* to be a father to a child.'

'That's why I told you that I was a superwoman, who could do it all on my own.'

'You knew?'

'Well, I had a fair idea you would be challenged.'

'And in the wrong mood, Pansy can be challenging, and I learned that I could cope the same way you do, with common sense and care. I don't feel as restless and dissatisfied with you in my life. I told you I couldn't do soppy.'

'And then you did the fireworks and the fab bath by candlelight and I thought, *Oh, yes, he can do anything he wants to do.* And you wanted to do it for me. It made me feel amazing.'

They strolled very slowly back to their wedding reception, but were so mutually absorbed that they really might as well not have bothered. That tight little pool of happiness enclosed them and closed out other people. A long time later, they went to bed and they talked and laughed and made love. The next day they travelled by road to join the yacht. Raj was set on Madagascar.

'Fabulous flora,' he promised her.

'I love you,' she told him fiercely, touched that he was always thinking of her interests, rather than his own.

'I'll love you for ever,' he swore passionately.

EPILOGUE

SIX YEARS LATER, Sunny rested back in the sunlight and contemplated her family as they played.

Pansy, a strikingly pretty little girl even at the age of seven, was presiding over the younger children in the family. She was a bossy boots and already obsessed with medicine. Since she showed every sign of having inherited her grandfather and uncle's intellect, it was likely that Pansy would eventually fulfil her ambition.

Kristof was five, pushing six, with a head of dark cropped hair and his mother's violet-blue eyes. He was a maths whizz like his father but he wanted to be a fireman. His little brother, Tamas, was three and he liked to paint on walls, if nothing else was available. He was a laid-back little boy otherwise, blond and brown-eyed. Pansy's long-desired little sister had finally been born the year before. Lili was dark and blue-eyed like her older brother Kristof and, now that she could crawl, she tried to follow Pansy everywhere. Pansy had found her little sister more of a liability than she had expected but also more fun. That was the family complete. Four children, all relatively close in age, were quite sufficient, Sunny reflected, simply grateful to have achieved the family she had always wanted without having the fertility problems she had feared would dog her.

They lived in London during the week and often spent weekends at Ashton Hall, where the children could run wild and participate in all the outdoor activities they enjoyed. Holidays invariably revolved round the yacht and visiting Raj's various properties. Sunny had discovered a very rare orchid on the Ashton estate and her painting of it now hung in the Royal Academy. She painted most days and their travels had influenced her art, for she now excelled at depicting more exotic flora than had once been to her taste. Raj, she had come slowly to recognise, had not clipped her wings. No, he had enhanced her ability to fly high and free.

She still wasn't very much into fashion and she still mislaid her specs everywhere she went. Raj still organised her but she had got used to it. She realised that she had never really known what it was to be happy until she had met him, and having found that happiness, she had at first been afraid to trust in it and had feared all the change and vulnerability that came with reaching for what she most wanted. But she had no regrets.

Raj striding out now to join their picnic, sheathed in well-worn jeans and an open shirt surveyed his family with pleasure. An elderly chihuahua, who had become like his little shadow followed his every step while Bear, who was much lazier, slumbered peacefully in the shade of the trees while keeping a careful eye on the children.

'Dad's here…*at last*,' Pansy exclaimed. 'Do you realise that Mum wouldn't let us eat until you arrived?'

Amused by that reproof, Sunny merely smiled. 'Family eats together.'

'I got stuck on the phone,' Raj sighed, dropping fluidly down beside Sunny on the rugs she had spread.

She was wearing something long and loose and swirly. It probably had a designer tag but it was still very much her style and she looked beautiful. Lili was steadily crawling towards him. Kristof, showing off, tried to execute a rugby save which sent Tamas flying and he burst into floods of overexcited tears. Sunny picked him up and planted a sandwich in his hand and he subsided before returning to the game with vigour. Lili finally reached Raj's knees and he swung her high and she giggled and giggled, her chubby little body convulsed with delight.

'If people will keep lifting her and carrying her, she'll never learn to walk,' Pansy lamented.

'She needs cuddled,' Raj countered. 'We all need cuddled now and again.'

'Mum's *always* cuddling you,' Pansy groaned in embarrassment.

Lili saw food and sat down clumsily to eat and Pansy dropped down beside her to help, pushing a toddler cup into her sibling's hand. Eventually they were all eating and quiet.

Raj poured Sunny wine and lay down beside her in the dappled sunlight. 'Tonight we will be alone in Paris,' he savoured. 'And you, my children, will have Maria and her assistants taking care of you.'

Sunny smiled even more widely because they spent their every anniversary alone in Paris and she got her fireworks and her fancy bath. Her dancing violet blue eyes met his level dark gaze in a moment of intense connection. She had never believed it possible to love anyone as much as she loved Raj. Or that anyone would ever look for her when she was absent and love her with the intensity that he did.

'Watch out…they're going to start kissing!' Pansy screwed up her face in disgust.

Raj's hand closed over Sunny's. 'Remind me again. Why did we decide we would have four of them?'

'You and Pansy needed more people to boss around.'

Her shapely body melted into the heat and hardness of his that night in Paris while she watched her fireworks from the balcony, exulting in the happiness flooding through her. 'I love you,' she murmured with her warm heart in her eyes.

He carried her back indoors to the big white linen draped bed and spread her across it with precision. He leant over her and kissed her until her heart was pounding. 'You are so loved, my precious Mrs Belanger.'

* * * * *